NICK

AGENT WEASEL

AND THE HIGHWAY HEDGEHOG

HODDER

THE UNITED WOODLANDS

W16 HQ

GARRET'S FARM

THE DITCH

SPOOKY HOLLOW

HEDGE HIGHWAY

THE CROSSROADS

HEDGE

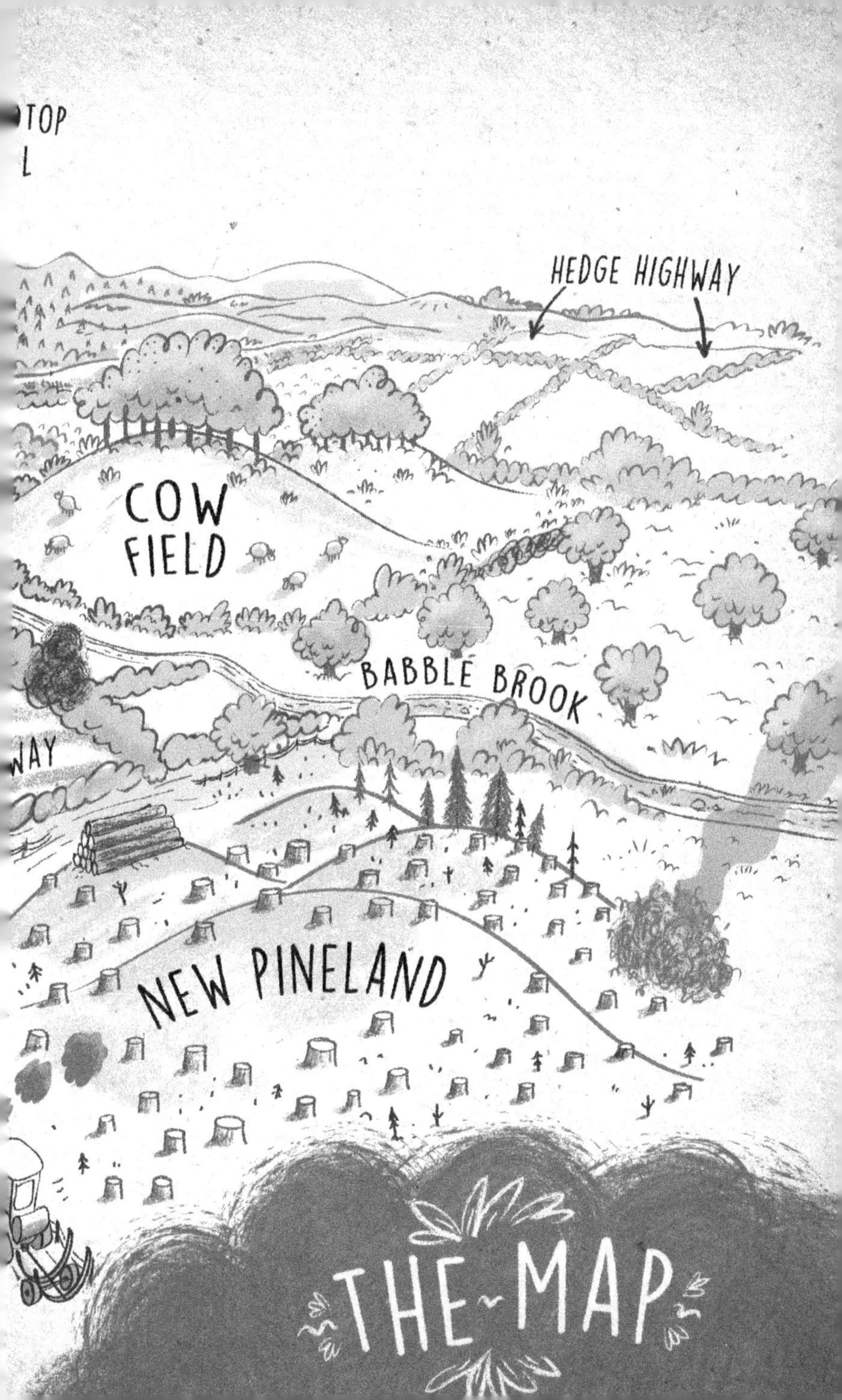

TOP
L

HEDGE HIGHWAY

COW
FIELD

BABBLE BROOK

WAY

NEW PINELAND

THE MAP

HODDER CHILDREN'S BOOKS

First published in Great Britain in 2023 by Hodder & Stoughton Limited

1 3 5 7 9 10 8 6 4 2

A CIP catalogue record for this book is available from the British Library.

ISBN 978 1 444 94528 7

Printed and bound in Great Britain by Clays Ltd, Elcograph S.p.A.
The paper and board used in this book are made from wood from
responsible sources

Hodder Children's Books
An imprint of Hachette Children's Group
Part of Hodder and Stoughton
Carmelite House
50 Victoria Embankment
London EC4Y 0DZ
An Hachette UK Company
www.hachette.co.uk
www.hachettechildrens.co.uk

THIS STORY IS FOR MY BROTHER TIM AND ALL
WHO HELPED MAKE THIS BOOK.
MAY YOUR JOURNEYS BE CALM, EASY
AND FREE OF NAUGHTY BANDITS.
WITH LOVE, NICK X

In a forgotten corner of the countryside lies a small green wood, much like any other. But take a closer look and it is far from ordinary. For this is the United Woodlands – home of Agent Weasel, legendary super-spy. A place full of adventure, mystery – and an incredibly wide variety of edible nuts.

PROLOGUE

SNAP, CRACK, CRUNCH, POP!

'AAAARGH! This stuff is just SOOOOO annoying,' fumed the little squirrel.

The night was inky black. And it was hard enough to see a paw in front of your whiskers, let alone the trail of dry-toasted leaves and twigs under your feet.

Bush-tail was her name – Nutter Bush-tail. Plucky special agent trainee for WI6, which stood for Woodland Intelligence, with a number six bunged on the end for no particular reason.

Her TOP SECRET mission? To escort WI6 head-honcho hedgehog H to New Pineland. Neighbouring wild place to the mighty United Woodlands. Her home, and home to Nutter's one and only hero, Agent Weasel. The greatest rootin'-tootin' spy the Woodlands had ever seen. Or so she thought, anyway. H seemed to think otherwise – she'd even mentioned the word 'twit', which Nutter thought very unfair. But Nutter kept her opinion to herself.

H waddled along behind the sprightly young squirrel, mumbling that she was 'just too old for this kind of thing'. Even Nutter had to admit, the going had been tough. Particularly as they'd now eaten all of their supplies. Especially the scrummy biscuits, the round ones with pink stripy icing on top. Nutter's favourites.

The pair were travelling by hedge, or the Hedge Highway, as it was known to all the animals. The safest way to get from one wild place to another. Much better than crossing an open field and getting snaffled by a fox. Or squished by a human farm-machine-thingy. Or worse still – falling face-first in a poopy cowpat.

But the summer had been very hot and dry. Everything crackled and crunched. And to top it all, prowling baddie-bandits had been spotted in the area. And here they were – making enough racket to wake a hibernating heffalump. Not that heffalumps actually exist, but if they did, they would have certainly woken it.

'WOOOO-HOO-HOO …'

Nutter jolted in shock at the sound of flapping above them and her cap popped off her head. Something rustled in a nearby tree.

'It's just an owl,' huffed H matter-of-factly.

Nutter gasped in relief. Did nothing spook this elderly hedgehog?

As the squirrel bent down to retrieve her cap, there came a sudden … SNAP!

'Ooooooh!' yelped H, grabbing on to the younger animal's fluffy tail.

Hmm, not so fearless after all, thought Nutter.

'Listen!' hissed H. There was a soft SNORT-SNORT-SNUFFLE-SNORT. Then a CRACK … a CRUNCH and a POP! It sounded like … paw-steps closing in! The Hedge Highway suddenly didn't feel all that safe any more.

At that moment, the moon peeked out from behind a cloud and its silvery light revealed a gap in the hedge and a cow-field beyond.

'Let's take our chance with the cowpats!' whispered Nutter urgently. She grabbed H by the paw, and they bolted for the opening. After only a couple of strides, something tight and stringy snagged against her leg.

What was that?

TWANG–WHOOSH–
BOING–THWUMP ...

In a flash, the ground shifted beneath them and the pair were dangling upside down from a branch.

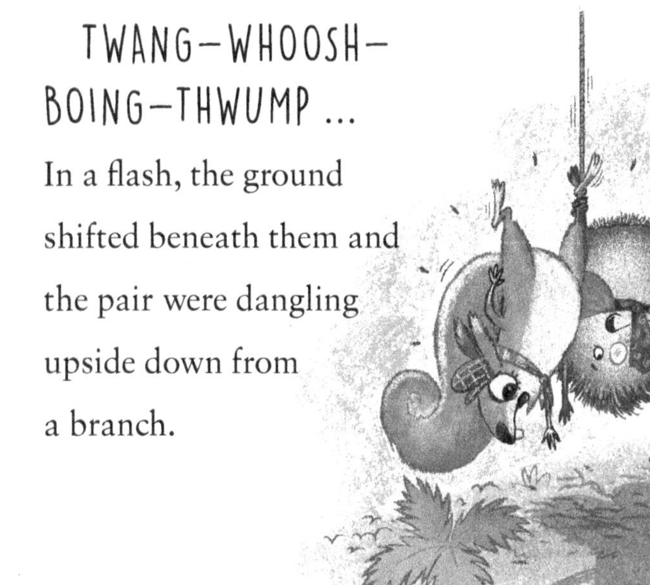

AAAARGH ... A PESKY TRAP! How did I fall for that? she scolded herself. Agent Weasel would be SOOOO disappointed. Just as she was about to flip upright and gnaw them free, a dark, round shadow waddled up. SNORT–SNORT–SNUFFLE–SNORT ... came the same noise as before, but this time it was followed by a haughty voice. 'STAND AND DELIVER!'

'Stand and WHAT?' asked H crossly. 'How are we supposed to *stand*? Can't you see that we're dangling?'

The figure stepped forward into the moonlight and Nutter gasped.

'N-no, not you ... it just c-c-can't be,' H cried.

'Ah, yes, my dear. You've been hog-tied – hedgehog-tied. Tarquin, bag 'em up.'

And before Nutter or H could utter a reply, everything went black.

CHAPTER 1

WEEEEE-OOOOOOO! WEEEEE-OOOOOOO! WEEEEE-OOOOOOOO!

Weasel blinked his eyes open. *What on earth is that terrible din? And why is it so dark?* And why did his ears tingle with frostbite and his toes feel like they were sizzling on a barbecue? It took a moment for Agent Weasel to remember where he was – lying in the garden, in a paddling pool, with an icebox stuck on his head. Well, of course he was.

While this might seem unusual to you and me, it was fairly normal stuff for Woodlands super-spy

Agent Weasel. Doing things by the book was just not his thing. Much to the annoyance of his boss, H, the head-honcho hedgehog at WI6. Who did *everything* by the book.

Thinking of H, he'd not heard anything from her or WI6 recently, which was strange. Usually, his super-spy hotline phone rang constantly! Plus, there'd been no sign of his new apprentice spy, Nutter Bush-tail. And just as he was getting used to having her around. Where on earth had everybody gone?

Maybe they were enjoying the summer heat too, he thought. He stretched out his long weaselly body, soaking up the late afternoon sun.

WEEEEE-OOOOOO! WEEEEE-OOOOOOO! WEEEEE-OOOOOOOO!

OOOOH! That annoying racket again; it sounded like an owl with a wonky hoot. He tried to yank the icebox free, but it refused to budge.

Nope, it was well and truly frozen on.

The box had contained Weasel's stash of lilac-fizz ice lollies – his favourites. But in true Weasel style, he had scoffed the lot in no time. And with this being the United Woodlands' hottest summer on record, who could blame him? Even cooling off with an icebox on your head seemed a perfectly reasonable thing to do, in this heat.

'DOORKINS! OH DOOOORKINS!' Weasel called.

Doorkins Dormouse, Weasel's best pal ever, had been pottering in the garden of Flaky-Bark Cottage all morning. Weasel's little mousey chum lived in the tree next to his top-secret home. And if anyone could save him from this tricky pickle, it was Doorkins.

But where on earth was his diddy sidekick?

As Weasel stepped from the paddling pool, the loud

WEEEEE–OOOOOO! WEEEEE–OOOOOOOO!

noise grew closer and closer.

Weasel braced himself ready for impact. But rather than the usual crash-bang-wallop stuff, there came a ... FLUMP and ...

'WEEE-OOOOOO, WEEE-Oooo,' went a faint but familiar voice somewhere near his feet.

'D-Doorkins?' Weasel called. With the icebox still on his head, he had to rely on his other senses.

Taking a careful step forward, he nudged his foot against a soft furry lump and then something grabbed his ankle.

'YEEOOW!' cried Weasel in shock. Unable to keep his balance, he thumped down on his bottom and the icebox shot off his head. 'Thank goodness for that,' he sighed.

Then ... WHOOSH! ... down it came again and ... BONK! ... bounced off his noggin and into the begonias. Which are big flouncy flowers, if you didn't know.

As the stars cleared before Weasel's eyes, he noticed his little mouse buddy in a heap near the paddling pool. The poor little fella looked exhausted. And no wonder, dashing about in this heat making siren noises at the top of his lungs.

Suddenly, Muriel Moth, Weasel's personally trained elite homing moth, fluttered down on his shoulder. Muriel was the best pet ever. Clever and brave, she'd got him out of some tricky old squeezes in the past.

Weasel gazed admiringly at the pretty pattern on her little wings and sighed. Ahh.

The moth glared at the woodland super-spy, pointing a wing urgently at the small, weary rodent.

'Holy molehills!' cried Weasel. 'Time to put my expert first-aid skills into action.'

'UMPH!' puffed the dinky insect as she rolled her eyes.

Some time ago he'd tried to fix Muriel's poorly wing – a delicate operation, as you can imagine. But he had become so tangled up in rolls of bandages, it took Muriel nearly three hours to unravel him. And with her poorly wing. Safe to say, Weasel's first-aid skills were not exactly expert.

'Fi-fi-fi ...' croaked Doorkins.

'Fine? Of course you'll be fine, my friend. First-aider Weasel is on the case!'

'Uuuuuh,' groaned the little mouse wearily.

'Ah-ha! I have just the thing!' Weasel knew exactly what he needed – the small bottle of smelling salts with a hint of badger poo that he always carried in his trusty WI6 spy pullover. It could bring round a fully grown bull with a single sniff, and knock it right back out again. Such was the power of badger poo.

'Oh, bothersome bum-thistles,' he sighed.

Of course, he didn't have his handy WI6 pullover on today. Instead, he wore a rather nifty maroon swimming costume, knitted by Granny Weasel. She'd kindly sewn the badge he'd received for completing a ten-metre doggy-paddle on the front, as well as useful pockets here and there. One of which was in the middle of his back! Her knitting could be quite weird at the best of times.

Looking around for something, anything to revive his dazed pal, Weasel's eyes fixed on the paddling pool.

'Ha! That'll do the trick.' He dipped a paw in the sun-warmed water and gently sprinkled it on his chum's face.

Nothing! Doorkins just sighed with his eyes half closed.

Next, Weasel grabbed a plant pot, tipped out the

frazzled pansies, dunked it in the water and ... SPLOSH. Straight into Doorkins's mush.

Still nothing – apart from a small gurgle!

HMMMM! Weasel, now a little tetchy, gripped on to the side of the pool and, with a great big groan, he tipped the whole thing right over on to his best chum ... SWOOOOSH! Muriel looked on in disbelief at the wave of pool water.

'Oops,' said Weasel, scratching his chin. *Maybe I've overdone it again.*

As he quickly went to haul his buddy from beneath the pool ... BOOP. A small lump popped up in the middle. Weasel froze; all was quiet for a second or two. Then …

'F-F-FIRE!' it squeaked loudly. The pool lurched towards the gate, SQUEEZED through and shot off into the woods with surprising speed.

'AAARRGGH … DOORKINS, don't you dare pop my pool!' Weasel cried. He took a deep breath and scarpered after his quickly disappearing pal.

CHAPTER 2

'WEEEEEEOOOOOO-WEEEEEEOOOOO-WEEEEEOOOOO,' howled Doorkins as he hurtled through the trees.

'WHOA, MY FRIEND, WHOA!' cried Weasel. The little dormouse couldn't half shift. He must have eaten all his porridge that morning!

Agent Weasel had a hunch what was going on here. This WEEEEOOOOO siren business was a new thing. But ever since Doorkins had joined the Woodland Anti-Fire Team, or WAFT for short, he'd been on edge.

The baking-hot summer had left the countryside a little bit dry and crispy. Wildfires had popped up all over the place. And WAFT desperately needed smoke detectors. With Doorkins able to sniff a burning cake from several miles away, he'd signed up at once.

But even the slightest whiff of smoke seemed to send the dormouse into a blind panic.

'Well, this is the fastest paddling pool I've ever chased,' Weasel chuckled to Muriel. She rode in the back pocket of his knitted bathing suit, unable to see a thing. Which was probably for the best as they now approached two very large and close together elm trees.

The mouse-propelled pool shot between the two trunks and squeezed with a loud THWOP! out the other side. Straight into a bunch of picnicking bunnies. 'OW! WATCH IT!'

Sandwiches and fairy cakes went everywhere. Agent Weasel followed Doorkins, reaching out to grab an airborne sarnie or two.

'Pardon me. Bit peckish!' he called, taking a quick bite.

'BLAAAARH! Raw carrot and lettuce!' He winced and spat the gross rabbit food out. When he looked up

once again, he saw Doorkins hurtling towards a large and particularly thorny bramble bush.

'Oh no! My pool!' he panicked. Launching himself off a log, Weasel sailed through the air and ... THUMP! ... landed straight on top of the bouncy inflatable.

But it was too late! The front of the pool had already hit the bramble bush and ... POP! ... they were suddenly spiralling up into the air.

HISSSSSSSSSSS ...

They flew in an uncontrollable zigzag over the treetops – high enough to see the fields and hedges beyond.

'W-WHERE AM I!?' howled Doorkins, jolting out of his panicked state only to find himself in an even more terrifying one.

'DON'T WORRY, OLD CHUM,' yelled Weasel over the loud hissing noise, 'I'LL HAVE US OUT OF THIS IN A JIFFY.'

Muriel raised her eyebrows doubtfully, seeing how floppy the pool had become.

SNIFF, SNIFF. Doorkins's eyes widened in horror. 'There's smoke, Weasel! Twelve o'clock!'

Twelve o'clock? Surely that meant it was time for lunch?

A grey column of smoke caught Weasel's attention. Ah! Clearly Doorkins had meant a fire lay straight ahead – not the actual time of day.

Clamping a paw either side of it, he began to lean and steer the speedily deflating pool.

SWOOOSH! They were suddenly out in the open above Little Thicket – capital of the United Woodlands.

It was then that Weasel spotted the figure. It looked like H, head-honcho hedgehog at WI6, but in the strangest of outfits. A kind of dandy pirate costume with an eye mask and cape. She watched them soar over, grinned widely and quickly waddled off into the bushes. *How odd*, Weasel thought.

'Weasel, turn now!' squeaked Doorkins urgently. Weasel snapped his head up – they were zooming directly towards a row of burning cottages, without doubt the cause of the smoke. But the pool was almost out of air and impossible to turn.

'Brace yourselves!' The super-spy winced. 'We're coming in hot.'

And they certainly were.

THUMP! CRASH! BOSH!

They fell through the roof and into the blazing building!

CHAPTER 3

'Oh no! We'll be burned to a crisp!' yelled Doorkins.

Muriel tucked her wings down inside Weasel's pocket. Scorched moth wings were a big no-no.

'Hold on!' cried Weasel over the roaring blaze. 'Something's moving!'

The deflated pool unexpectedly launched a few feet into the air.

'Eh?' puzzled Weasel. Then with a soft thump, they landed again. Then up, then ... THUMP! back down.

'We're b-b-bouncing?' Doorkins yelped.

'Well, bake my potatoes! I believe we are, my friend,' Weasel exclaimed.

'Oi! I can't see a fing!' came a deep, gruff voice from beneath the punctured pool.

'Oh, we're awfully sorry,' replied Weasel.

'WILL YOU GET OFF?' growled the sizeable lump. 'I'VE GOT AN IMPORTANT JOB TO DO 'ERE!'

'Er … we can't,' replied Weasel. 'I'm afraid we'll be turned into animal fries if we do.'

'Fair enough! You'd better point my behind in the right direction, then,' it bellowed.

'Pardon – point your what?' Weasel asked, rather surprised.

'MY BOTTOM! I NEED TO PUT OUT THESE FLAMES WITH MY BOTTOM!'

Weasel still wasn't sure he understood but he had heard stranger things in his line of work. 'Er ... OK,' replied Weasel.

'If you could just shift ... left a bit ... A bit more ...' Weasel guided. But they suddenly bounced in the opposite direction. Of course, Weasel's left would be *their* right.

'No! I mean right! Go right, right!' he called. And they instantly bounded left, left, left ... and straight into another unsuspecting bottom bouncer, who flew right through a nearby wall!

'OI! WHAT'S GOING ON?' thundered the voice below.

Weasel had never been good with directions –

particularly under pressure. The fire roared louder and flames climbed higher.

'AAAAARGH! We're going to be frazzled!' squealed Doorkins. But without warning … SWOOOOOOOSH! SPLOSH! HISSSSSSSSSSS.

The fire was out and they were soaked through to the skin.

'Well, if it doesn't rain it pours.' Weasel shrugged, water dripping from the end of his snout.

'I'm not sure that's quite the saying, or that was actually rain,' said Doorkins, wringing out a floppy ear.

As they looked up, a large white owl zoomed overhead.

With a loud WHOOSH, a big water balloon dropped from its talons and burst, putting out the remaining fire.

'Hurrah!' they cheered. It could only be Owl Force 1, the Woodlands' top flying squadron and all-round feathery good guys. With their goggles and leather flying caps, they were easy to spot.

'Well, they've only gone and saved the day.' Weasel beamed.

'Those owls always get the credit,' sighed a looming shape, appearing through the smoke.

Weasel and Doorkins looked up from a wet heap on the ground.

It was a badger. A huge, soggy, miserable-looking badger. With the most incredibly large – er – bottom they'd ever seen.

'Firefighter Babs of the Beefy Badger Brigade,' she introduced herself.

Of course! How could Weasel forget the Beefy Badger Brigade!? Brave animals, prepared to bounce out fires with their incredibly large backsides. They were proper heroes!

She dragged Weasel's punctured paddling pool in one paw, with a slightly charred picture frame in the other.

'Nice to meet you, Babs. What do you have there?' he asked politely.

'Paddling pool,' she replied.

'No, the other paw.' Weasel pointed.

'Oh! I found it back there,' replied the badger, sulkily waving a paw back at the smoking building. The frame held a photo.

'Wait a minute! Th-th-that's a picture of my granny ... GRANNY WEASEL!'

An odd, achy feeling suddenly appeared in his chest. He looked back at the burning house. The fire was out but what was left of the house – which wasn't very much at all – suddenly looked incredibly familiar. He hadn't noticed from the air, and when they'd landed, the smoke had covered everything. This was, or had been, where Granny Weasel lived! She was an Old Age Critter, OAC for short, and this smoking wreck was the retirement home she lived in!

'NO! Not Granny Weasel,' Weasel wailed mournfully. 'SHE WAS THE BEST GRANNY EVER!'

Well, apart from her weird ideas on knitting, her stinky dried mushroom collection and never being able to remember his name. Even though it was just 'Weasel'.

The super-spy buried his head and sobbed. BOO-HOO-HOO.

CHAPTER 4

A sudden commotion came from the village green.

'You'd better take a look, Weasel!' said Doorkins, patting his friend's arm.

There, perched on an old tree stump, was the one, the only Granny Weasel!

'If I need a bandage, I will jolly well ask for one!' she grumbled, batting a poor first-aid goose with her handbag.

'Granny! You're alive?' Weasel called as he dashed up. Granny Weasel stopped swinging her handbag – much to the goose's relief.

'Oooooh ... it's ... er ... what's-his-name?' she puzzled.

'It's me! Your grandson Weasel, Agent Weasel,' he replied, a little ruffled.

'Yes, that's right, A.J. Wuzzel,' she said. 'Of course, dear.'

'Really!' Weasel sighed, raising his eyes skyward.

FLAP! FLAP! FLAP! A broad, handsome barn owl swooped down to land nearby.

'Hello, Granny Weasel! Good day all, don't you know?' it boomed cheerfully.

Granny Weasel went all shy, fluttered her eyelashes and let out a small giggle Weasel had never heard before. 'Ooooh ... if it isn't that polite, handsome owl, Captain Barney-Barnster.'

'Ah, pleasure, ma'am, don't you know?' He saluted with a quick flick of his wing.

'So, she can remember HIS name!' Poor Weasel gawped.

But Weasel couldn't stay cross for long. Barney-Barnster was a top fellow and Owl Force 1's best flyer. He'd even saved Weasel's bacon on their last adventure. But he did have this annoying habit of saying 'don't you know?' at the end of each sentence. And it was catching.

‘Weasel, old chap! We need a bit of an urgent chinwag, don’t you know?’ he whispered secretively from behind a huge wing.

‘But what about my feeble old granny … don’t you know?’ Oh no, he’d got Weasel doing it now.

‘Don’t you fret, Mr Weasel,’ honked the first-aid goose cheerfully. ‘We’ll look after your gran—OOOF!’ Granny Weasel had landed another blow on the goose’s head.

‘I can look after myself perfectly well, thank you,’ she snapped.

‘Right … We’ll be off then, Granny. Important WI6 business, don’t you know?’ said Weasel, trying to slink away.

She looked up blankly.

‘Er, oh yes. Bye, erm, A.J.-what’s-it.’

Weasel groaned. *Well, at least the old dear’s safe*, he thought to himself. *Not so sure about that goose*, *though*. Sounds of the kerfuffle faded as Weasel and Captain Barney strolled off.

'The United Woodlands needs help, old chap.' Barney-Barnster frowned. 'These fires are getting a little out of—'

'Paw?' offered Weasel.

'I was going to say "wing", don't you know?' He shrugged.

'Ah, of course,' said Weasel.

'A lot of ears, paws and tails getting singed,' continued the large bird. 'And as for the poor Beefy Badger Brigade—'

'It's true,' interrupted Firefighter Babs, appearing out of thin air. 'We're working all hours and my comrades' poor scorched bottoms are on their last, er, legs.'

'Hmmm,' pondered Weasel. 'What about those famous firefighting experts in New Pineland? You

know, the ones with the funny name?'

'FAFFS?' questioned Doorkins, who'd been listening carefully in the background. Babs tried not to giggle.

'Fearless Animal Fire-Fighting Squadron – FAFFS for short,' replied the little mouse. Babs tried not to giggle again.

'Well, they sound perfect,' exclaimed Barney-Barnster, turning to Weasel. 'Could you maybe pop over to New Pineland, grab a bunch of firefighting experts and pop back here lickety-split, don't you know?'

Weasel's eyes bulged. New Pineland was not just a pop away – it was *miles*. And the only way was through Garrett's farmyard, which meant facing Mrs Fluffykins, the dreaded farm moggie. Not to mention Oi the sheepdog – who was pretty much deaf as a post, but still!

'Er ...' Weasel pondered uncertainly.

'Good show, old man! I knew you'd be up for it, don't you know?' Barney-Barnster nearly knocked him flat with a great big friendly whack on the back.

'Well, Doorkins, I guess we'd best break out the old adventure kit, eh,' he said, realising he was probably ready for another daring mission.

But why wasn't H telling him all this? She was head honcho after all. What on earth was she doing flouncing about in the woods with a silly costume on?

'Well, good luck, old chap. And, er ... one thing, Agent: watch out for the bandits, don't you know?' And with that he took off. Literally.

'Did he say bandits?' puzzled Doorkins.

'No, I'm sure it was sand-nits' replied Weasel. Muriel frowned. 'Nippy little things, don't you know?' Prickly bum-thistles, he'd just said it again.

CHAPTER 5

Night had fallen as Agent Weasel, Doorkins and Muriel made their way to the very edge of the United Woodlands, known as the Ditch! Because it was a … erm … ditch. Beyond that lay Garrett's Farm and Mrs Fluffykins the farmyard cat. Gulp!

Weasel took a deep breath, pushing the ferocious feline to the back of his mind.

He had swapped his swimming costume for his trusty old spy pullover and also carried a special WI6 survival rucksack that contained many useful things. Most importantly, *The Big Bumper Book*

THE
DITCH

of Survival. It had all the survival skills an animal could need. It even showed how to whittle stuff from wood, including cutlery, cups and even a coffee table! This made Weasel very excited and ready to whittle any old thing.

'How do we get across this?' whispered Doorkins, trying not to wake any scary farmyard beasts. He stood staring down into the ditch, as Muriel fluttered over from Weasel's pocket to perch on his head. She wrinkled her mothy nose at the ditch's pongy whiff, most likely caused by the gungy green sludge creeping along its bottom.

After a few moments of pondering and stroking his chin, Weasel yelled, 'I have an idea!'

'Shh,' shushed Doorkins. 'Not so loud, Weasel.'

'Sorry, old chum,' whispered the super-spy. He pulled out a small penknife and bounded off into the woods.

CHIFF-CHIFF-CHIFF-CHIFF went the unmistakeable sound of whittling, coming from Weasel's direction. Doorkins and Muriel looked at each other, baffled. After a little while, he came bouncing back with a long, finely whittled pole.

'Impressive, Weasel. But what's it for?' questioned the dormouse.

'Isn't it obvious, old chum?' said Weasel with a determined look. 'We're going to pole-vault across.'

'Are you sure that's a good idea?' said Doorkins, rather concerned. But Weasel had already paced back into the woods for a run-up. Muriel covered her eyes as he raised the pole and ran. DUFF, DUFF, DUFF, DUFF ... THUNK-SPLOTCH. The pole stuck into

the bottom of the ditch and up Weasel flew. The mouse and moth watched on in amazement – it was actually working!

But then … BOING! The pole waggled to a halt, halfway across.

'Ah! I have a bad feeling about this.' Weasel cringed. They watched helplessly as Weasel slowly slid down the pole and, with a soft squelch, into the manky ditch below. Muriel tittered behind her wing and Doorkins struggled not to laugh at the comical sight.

'Someone's coming!' hissed Doorkins, ears twitching.

The small mouse flattened himself on the ground

and Muriel fluttered to a nearby tree.

But poor Agent Weasel had nowhere to go! So he slunk down further into the muck until just his eyes peeked out from the gluey sludge.

A dark, round shadow silently waddled to the edge of the ditch. Weasel struggled to hold his breath. But as he strained, a small bottom squeak escaped and bubbled to the surface. GURGLE, GURGLE, it went. The shadow froze and two glowing beady eyes turned on the WI6 spy, as a long blade of grass tickled his nose and … uh-oh. He couldn't hold it in! BLAAAAAAAAAAH! He sneeze-snorted the gunk out through his snout, loud enough to alert every animal

in the United Woodlands. *Oh no, I've blown it now!* he thought. But, strangely, the shadow didn't move an inch.

'Weasel, old bean, is that you?' A torch clicked on and a familiar face appeared.

'Agent Mole!' Weasel squeaked in relief.

'In a bit of a pickle again, my friend?' she said cheerfully. Mole was a jolly old sort, top WI6 spy, expert digger and all-round good egg. She reached down a large spade-like paw and dragged Weasel from the gloop with ease.

'Thanks, Mole,' he said gratefully. 'What in wobbly-walnut's-name are you doing out here?'

Mole wrinkled her nose at the ditchy pong wafting off her WI6 comrade.

'Well, I was at home with my paws up doing nothing so I thought I'd come out for a stroll.' She shrugged. 'That's when I heard all the commotion.'

Hmm, wondered Weasel. Why was a top agent like Mole sitting with her feet up? Why were the spy hotlines not ringing? What was H up to?

'Do you think the … bridge might have been a better idea?' Mole asked gently, pointing to a small crossing further down. Doorkins and Muriel tried not to snigger. Poor old Weasel, after all that effort whittling as well!

'Righto, let's be off!' Weasel blurted out a little awkwardly. 'We've got a farmyard to cross.'

'And a bridge,' tittered Doorkins. Weasel smiled. Despite being covered in muck, he guessed it was just a *little* funny.

Whilst the others made off towards the bridge, Weasel found a tufty patch of grass and flopped down to roll off the gungy mess.

He sat up, squinting into the dark. He thought he'd heard something; perhaps it was the sound of his own rolling around. But then … SNAP! went a twig. Someone was there! He squinted into the dark and made out a round, bulky shadow just ahead.

'Oh, Mole, it's just you. I'll just be two ticks,' he said lying back down. When Mole didn't answer, he sat up again and reached for his torch, flicking it on.

Walloping willow trees!

'You're not Mole!' Weasel fumbled the torch in surprise and with a CLICK! the light went out.

CHAPTER 6

Weasel fumbled around in the dark, trying to locate the torch.

Had it really been H, WI6 head-honcho hedgehog?

Am I seeing things now? he thought. Maybe the toxic ditch gunge had sent him a little doolally?

A rustle in the grass made Weasel look up. CRIKEY! There it was again! A dark, round shadow waddled towards him.

'HA! Now I've got you!' he cried, flicking on the torch once again.

But it wasn't H who stood in the beam of light – it was Agent Mole.

'Yikes!' she gasped. 'You gave me a fright.'

'Sorry, Mole, but I thought I just saw ...' Weasel stopped. Did he want Mole to think he was completely cuckoo? Had he really just seen H in that dandy pirate costume again?

'Problem, Weasel?' questioned Mole.

'No ... no, Mole. All tip-top,' he fibbed a bit. Mole looked a little uncertain. But they gathered themselves together and scampered off towards the farm gate.

All seemed quiet in the farmyard. For a moment, the house lights flicked on upstairs, but they went straight back out again.

'I think Farmer Garrett has gone beddy-byes,' whispered Mole with a grin.

'Hope they've had their hot chocolate,' said

CLACKERTY
CLACK
WATER TROUGH

Doorkins longingly – wishing he was at home sipping a mug in his own bed.

'Come on, let's go,' said Weasel, keen to dash across the farmyard without a thought. But Mole held him back.

CLACKETY, CLACK, CLACK ... came a noise from the nearby house.

'Sounds like a c-c-cat flap!' Doorkins trembled.

Mole reached into her WI6 survival rucksack and pulled out a rather flash pair of binoculars.

'Night vision, with firefly technology,' she whispered proudly. Two little fireflies popped out, gave a thumbs up, then popped back in again. *Hmmm, why haven't I got a pair of those?* thought Weasel enviously.

Mole scanned the yard for any sign of movement.

'Yep, just as I thought,' she said, handing the binoculars over to Weasel, who'd just remembered

– he could already see quite well in the dark. As weasels can. *Mind you, I still wouldn't mind a pair of these bad boys*, he thought.

There, creeping steadily towards the barn, was the one and only … MRS FLUFFYKINS. A shudder went down Weasel's back. This kitty was famous for being mean and sneaky – not to mention her impressive set of razor-sharp claws.

Mind you, she *was* quite cute and fluffy – if you liked that sort of thing.

'Mewling moggies, we've just missed our chance,' groaned Weasel. Doorkins frowned.

'Hold on, my friends,' said Mole. She studied a rather smart WI6 spy watch on her wrist. *How did she get all this cool spy stuff?* thought Weasel sulkily.

'Don't worry, this kitty is as regular as clockwork,' she said, the watch lighting up her face. 'She'll be round the back of that barn in ... five ... four ... three ... two ... one!'

And Fluffykins slunk out of sight – just as Mole said!

'Brilliant! Off we go, then!' Weasel took a deep breath, ducked under the gate and scampered across the yard. The others followed. They reached a rusty old tin bathtub with the words 'water trough' painted on the side in wonky letters.

Doorkins pricked up an ear. 'Hear that?' he whispered, just as a low rumbling rolled around the yard.

'Sorry,' Weasel said, holding his tummy. 'I missed

my supper.' But his little chum shook his head, pointing to a rickety doghouse nearby. Two large paws poked out of the front, a big wet nose and a grumbling snore not far behind.

It could only be Oi, the farm guard dog, who appeared to be completely out of it. Not much of a guard dog, if you asked Weasel.

'Where to next?' Mole asked, looking uncertainly at the snoozing dog.

Weasel swept the yard with his night-vision eyes. A blue tractor stood some way off, facing the barn.

And ... was that ...? It couldn't be. If Weasel's eyes weren't deceiving him, the all-too-familiar

shadow of H had reappeared, this time peeking out from behind the tractor's big rear wheels.

'Everything all right, Weasel?' asked Doorkins, seeing the befuddled look on his friend's face.

'Do you see—' he began to reply, but when he looked again, the shadow was gone. It was official, he'd gone totally barmy.

As they were about to make a move for the tractor, a loud grating noise came from the farmhouse window.

'CHITTER-CHITTER-CHAT-CHAT-CHAT.'

GULP! Weasel knew that dreaded call all too well. He looked up.

There, sitting in a cage on a high windowsill, was the ROBBER KING, Granny Garrett's pet magpie. This bird was a bit of a rotter and had caused all sorts of bother in Weasel's last adventure (see *Agent Weasel and the Robber King* in all good bookshops). The super-spy had managed

CHITTER—CHITTER
CHAT—CHAT

to put him back behind bars – but now it looked like he wanted revenge!

'CHITTER-CHITTER-CHAT-CHAT-CHAT!' he called again, glaring at Weasel with a cruel smirk. Crikey, he was going to wake the whole farm.

'Ssso, who do we have here then?' came a silky hiss from above their heads. The friends slowly craned their necks upwards, where a large pair of scarily familiar green eyes stared over the edge of the bath!

'M-M-MRS FLUFFYKINS!' squeaked Doorkins in terror.

'Nice to meet you, little mousssssse,' said the cat, eyeing Doorkins hungrily.

This moggie was terrifying and very far from cute and fluffy. *Better turn on the super-spy charm*, thought Weasel, *or we'll all end up being this kitty's dinner*.

'Ahem, h-hello, madam,' he said shakily. 'Having a g-good evening?'

'Well, I ssss-certainly am now that supper has sss arrived,' replied the cat.

Weasel, Agent Mole and Doorkins gulped – even Muriel gulped a little. And moths don't normally gulp. Fluffykins raised her bottom and waggled, getting ready to pounce.

To Weasel's surprise, Agent Mole stepped out in front of the coiled cat.

'Mole, no!' he cried, fearing for his friend's life.

The WI6 spy aimed a clenched paw upwards and pressed a button on her WI6 wristwatch.

SQUIRRRRT!

A jet of water went straight into Fluffykins's fluffy face.

'MEEEEEOOOWW!' she howled, scrabbling around on the edge of the bathtub. But even her claws couldn't keep a grip. And with a loud SPLASH! in she went.

'Wow! I've got to get me one of those,' Weasel exclaimed.

'It also has a toothpick and a corkscrew!' Mole beamed smugly.

Mrs Fluffykins thrashed around in the bath, making a terrible din. And then, the magpie started up again … 'CHITTER-CHITTER-CHAT-CHAT-CHAT.'

'Time we were off!' said Weasel. The team dashed for the blue tractor. 'Eek!' yelped Doorkins, tripping over a stray rope that was attached to Oi's collar. With a jolt, the dog woke instantly.

'WOOF! WOOF! WOOF!'

'CHITTER-CHATTER-CHAT-CHAT!'

'MEEEEEOOOOW!'

What a hullabaloo! The farmhouse lights flickered on.

Farmer Garrett was awake!

'Quick, Doorkins!' Weasel grabbed the mouse by his paw.

Racing towards the tractor, they scuttled up a big, knobbly tyre and on to the seat. And only just in time. Oi chomped and slobbered below, straining on his rope.

'Now what?' said Mole, nervously looking down at the dog's gnashing teeth.

Weasel, short of ideas, began to frantically fiddle with the tractor's levers and buttons. Doorkins raised an eyebrow. 'Do you think that's a good idea, Wea—?'

CLUNK! Weasel had already pushed a red lever, and the tractor began to roll forward!

'Hmm ... I was kind of hoping for an ejector seat,' said Weasel, a little disappointed.

Then he realised the tractor was trundling straight for the barn. Mole, Doorkins and Muriel froze in wide-eyed shock as the tractor began to pick up speed.

CLUNK
YIKES
RUMBLE

'Chaps ... chaps ... CHAPS!' yelled the super-spy, clapping his paws together in a panicked frenzy. Muriel suddenly came to her senses and darted up in the air.

'We'll have to jump for it!' Weasel instructed firmly. Doorkins and Mole looked awfully unsure. Grasping his unwilling friends by the paws, the super-spy barked, 'On three! One ... two ... three ... JUMP!'

CRUUUUUNCH! They landed just as the tractor drove straight into the barn. The entire thing slowly collapsed inwards, in a cloud of splinters and dust.

'What is that awful pong?' Mole sniffed as she came out of her daze.

'Er ... I think that might be us,' replied Doorkins.

They had made a soft landing but, unfortunately, that soft landing happened to be slap bang in the middle of a big, stinky pile of manure, made even smellier by the hot weather!

'Oh great, that's the end of yet another spy pullover,' said Weasel sadly. He had the unfortunate habit of messing up his jumpers. Good job he had a cupboard full of them back at Flaky-Bark Cottage.

Suddenly, the farmhouse door swooshed open and the noisy animals fell silent. A big, bulky figure stood framed by the light. It could only be ... Farmer Garrett!

Weasel had seen him before – mostly from a distance, tootling about on his tractor. His tractor that now sat covered in what was left of the barn! But now, up close, he looked awfully big and scary. The enormous human stepped from the door and thumped down the steps.

'Oh no! How do we get out of this one?' trembled Doorkins.

'This way! Quickly!' whispered a faceless voice from behind the muck heap.

The animals looked at each other uncertainly.

Mole shrugged. 'Either we stay here and get snaffled by Oi and spotted by Garrett. Or we take our chances back there.' She nodded to the hedge behind the manure pile.

'What are we waiting for?' Weasel nodded eagerly. He dared a quick glance over his shoulder as they scampered off. A puzzled Farmer Garrett fished the bedraggled moggie out of the water. Mrs Fluffykins locked eyes with the woodland spy and scowled a

'jusssst you wait' kind of look. Weasel returned a friendly little wave. The cat's eyes widened with rage and she scrabbled and scratched to get at him. Farmer Garrett lost his grip on the slippery moggie as she swiped at his hands. And she promptly fell back into the trough with a loud SPLOSH!

As they entered the shadowy hedge, he could still hear the poor kitty's howls echo around the farmyard.

CHAPTER 8

They followed the dark figure as it bounded through the Hedge Highway at speed – leaping and dodging foliage as it went. This fellow had skills! The three friends struggled to keep up.

'Er, excuse me?' called Weasel. But the nimble creature raced on.

As they burst into a moonlit clearing, the who – or what – came to an abrupt halt. And so did Doorkins and Mole – careening straight into Weasel's back. THUMP! BUMP! CRASH!

'Ugh! Thanks for the h-help,' Weasel groaned from a heap on the floor when the dark figure made no move towards them.

Mole flicked on her torch. Their rescuer had their back to them – but it was a strangely familiar back. And then the animal turned.

'I don't believe it! NUTTER? NUTTER BUSH-TAIL?' gasped the super-spy.

'Weasel, I am so, so sorry about this,' she blubbered.

'Sorry about what, old chu—?'

WHOOSH! THWUMP! WHACK! The three friends suddenly found themselves hanging in a net, above the ground.

'A JOLLY ROTTEN TRAP!' fumed Mole.

'But Nutter ... WHY?' asked Weasel, surprised at the betrayal. Before Nutter could answer, a round shape waddled from the shadows.

'STAND AND DELIVER!' it ordered briskly.

'Pardon?' puzzled Weasel. They certainly couldn't stand, dangling as they were. And deliver what? A speech? A pizza ...? (He really wanted his supper.)

'Oh, never you mind,' huffed the round shape. 'It's just something we ... highway animals like to say.' And it stepped out into the moonlight.

'BLITHERING BANDICOOTS!' exclaimed Weasel. 'It's ... it's ... H, head-honcho hedgehog!'

She wore the same flouncy pirate costume he'd seen earlier that day. The WI6 boss had gone BADDIE!

'How very dare you!' H snapped. 'I am the HIGHWAY HEDGEHOG, scourge of the hedgerows, menace of the field edges, plague of the—' Her rant came to an abrupt halt as a stoat skulked out and whispered in her ear. The hedgehog gave a curt nod and cleared her throat.

'Ahem ... I believe it is time for my nap,' she said stiffly. 'I can become terribly grouchy if I don't get a snooze.'

Weasel raised his eyebrows. *Typical H*, he thought.

'Get this lot off to Spooky Hollow – quick smart,' said the highway honcho.

Hmm, Spooky Hollow? That's a well dodgy spot! thought Weasel. Known for bandits, rogues and ne'er-do-wells.

DOH! *Bandits*, not *sand-nits* – Captain Barney-Barnster *had* tried to warn him!

Suddenly, the hedge began to rustle and a gang of shifty-looking critters stalked out. They grabbed the net and, in the blink of an eye, the three friends were slung from a pole. It was carried by two rather skinny and ropey-looking ferrets.

'What's this lot been eatin'?' said one.

'Don't know, but they must 'ave 'ad a lot of it,' said the other, straining under the weight.

SNIFF–SNIFF. ''Ere, they don't half stink too!'

'Yer right! They smell like cow plop!'

'What rude and ragged ruffians!' snapped Mole. Weasel had to agree. Didn't this lot realise he had an important mission to complete? And now to top it all, H and Nutter had gone all rotten – what a mess!

The journey to Spooky Hollow was incredibly uncomfortable. It was all paws, legs and tails, tangled and crushed. Weasel, who was stuck awkwardly at the bottom of the net, managed to pull out his *Big Bumper Book of Survival*.

'Hmm. Surely there must be something on how to escape from a net-trap?' he murmured, flicking through the pages. 'Let me see ... How to whittle an egg-cup? No. How to whittle a birdbath? No! How to whittle a footstool? Close, but also no.'

To be honest, it was all mainly whittling – not a single thing about escaping from nets.

WIGGLY WOOD SHAVINGS, that was it! Whittling *was* the answer after all! He had the small penknife in the rucksack front pocket. Just the thing for cutting through bothersome nets.

But as much as Weasel tried, he couldn't quite reach the bag. Urgh!

Doorkins, always ready to help, stretched over and wiggled a paw into the rucksack pocket. He fiddled around a moment and pulled out a pair of nail clippers and held it up for Weasel, who shook his head. Doorkins rummaged again … and out came a nail file. Weasel shook his head. Next, a bottle of nail polish!

'Well, got to keep the old claws pretty.' Weasel grinned sheepishly.

The little mouse sighed heavily and delved in again. This time, with a bit more of a scrabble, he plucked out … yes! The penknife!

'Cut the net, my friend! Cut the net!' whispered

Weasel from the side of his mouth.

'OI, SHUT IT!' yelled one of the ferrets. 'What do you fink this is, an afternoon tea party?' Then it started to pick its nose.

'Urgh! Disgusting animal.' Mole winced.

Weasel nudged his dormouse buddy, urging him to get on with it.

Doorkins didn't like knives one bit. Who did? They were sharp and dangerous. But this one was so small and blunt, he thought he'd give it a go.

As he began to saw away, the ferret who was busy picking his nose didn't see the thick branch blocking his path up ahead and tripped.

The friends and the two bandits clattered to the ground in one big, jumbled heap.

Doorkins quickly gave his head a good shake and unclenched his paw. Oh no! Where had the penknife gone? He must have dropped it!

CHAPTER 9

'What on earth is going on back there?' called the Highway Hedgehog grumpily.

'Nofing, boss! Just a little accident,' said the ferret, scowling at his comrade.

Then he noticed something glint in the moonlight. He picked it up off the ground.

'Will you look at that!' he said greedily. 'It's a little shiny penknife'

'It's mine,' said the other ferret enviously. 'I dropped it when I tripped.'

'Why, you big fibber!' the first ferret replied.

They began to squabble, spitting and scratching viciously, while Weasel fumed. That was his best whittling knife! His only whittling knife, come to think of it.

He could feel a Weasel War Dance brewing. This is when a weasel is threatened or angry and loses its temper! A Weasel War Dance usually involves anything from wild bottom shaking to knocking your opponent flat with a single blow, so it's best not to be on their wrong side when they unleash it. But Weasel was stuck in a net with his friends and he didn't want to accidentally hurt them, so decided a Weasel War Dance would not be wise. Taking a deep breath, he tried to calm himself down.

'OUCH!' The ferrets cried out in unison as the hedgehog leader had stomped over, cuffed the pair of ferrets round the head, and held them each by an ear.

'I'm taking this,' she said, snatching the penknife. 'Both of you see me outside my leaf pile lodge, after my nap.'

'Aw, boss,' they moaned.

'Don't you "aw, boss" me! And neither of you will be seeing this again.' She looked at the knife in her paw, then snapped her head round to give Weasel a suspicious look. He thought about asking for it back – probably not the best idea – but before he could utter a word, off she went. She marched back to the front of the column, her cape swishing in the night air. The two grumbling ferrets hauled the net back up, and trudged on towards Spooky Hollow.

Poor Weasel's journey had become even more impossible now. Before Doorkins lost the knife, he'd managed to cut a fair-sized hole through the net. But unfortunately, the hole was only big enough for the super-spy's bum to drop through.

Now his sore behind scraped along the floor, catching every bump and thorny twig along the way. He groaned. This was going to be a long, painful ride back to the bandits' lair.

Suddenly, something tickled Weasel's face.

'Muriel!' He beamed with delight at the sight of his tiny friend. The clever little moth had managed to dodge the trap, small enough to flitter in and out of the small holes in the net.

'Eek!' he yelled as his bottom dragged over a particularly spiky thistle.

'Shut it!' warned one of the ferrets.

Weasel didn't know how much more his bum could take.

'Please g-get help, my little beauty,' he said wearily. Muriel snapped a winged salute and fluttered away. Weasel felt better, knowing his diddy homing moth was on the case.

As the group made their way through the hedge, Weasel could see Nutter Bush-tail up ahead. *What in crab-apples' name is she doing?* he fumed silently. The little squirrel walked alongside baddie H, like she was part of the highway gang. She would need a stern telling-off when he got the chance – *if* he got the chance!

'Weasel, look!' whispered Mole urgently. A large, creepy tree loomed through a gap in the hedge. Something appeared to be fluttering around its crown but exactly what, he couldn't tell.

They arrived at an opening between the hedges. The large tree stood in the centre; its trunk was the widest Weasel had ever seen. It had what looked like an opening at its base. But the branches were the weirdest thing, going off in all sorts of strange directions. It looked like a giant, monstrous spider. This could only be the infamous Spooky Hollow!

SPOOKY
HOLLOW

'B-B-BATS! Horrible, leathery BATS!' yelped Doorkins, pointing a trembling paw upwards.

Flapping and fluttering around the top of the great tree were hundreds of diving, dodging black shapes. These were the little mouse's least favourite animal of all.

'Oh, I don't know, Doorkins,' Weasel reassured. 'I've known some very nice bats in my time.'

SPLAT! A big plop of runny bat poo landed right on Weasel's head. He frowned. 'But not these ones, it would seem.'

THUMP! OOOF! The friends were dropped to the ground.

'Ooh ... glad to get that lot off me back,' groaned the relieved ferret.

'Ugh! Why does it smell like a farmyard around here!?' griped the uppity hedgehog as she waddled up with Nutter Bush-tail.

'If you'd fallen in a muck pile, wouldn't you smell like—' began Mole.

'That's enough!' barked the boss bandit. The WI6 agent crossed her arms in a huff. 'After my well-deserved nap, I demand to hear all about your little ... mission,' she said, narrowing her eyes at them before turning to the ferrets. 'Take them away!'

One of the ferrets hooked a dangly rope to the top of the net. And then, with its shifty partner, began to haul the friends upwards.

Oh no! We're heading straight for the

hordes of swarming bats, thought Weasel. He glanced over at Doorkins, hoping his little mouse buddy didn't notice—

'NOOOOO!' cried Doorkins, looking up at the fluttering mass. Too late!

CHAPTER 10

As the net drew nearer to the frantic bats, the more nervous poor Doorkins became.

'They're going to eat us, they're going to eat us!' he yelped.

'Honestly, buddy, they wouldn't hurt a fly,' said Weasel, trying to calm his rodent friend.

THWUMP! A small black nugget suddenly crashed into the net.

'Well, actually, I would,' chirped a little bat, clinging on by its tiny claws. 'I scoff at least three thousand a day.'

'What!? You eat THREE THOUSAND d-dormice every day?' Doorkins quaked, looking close to passing out.

'No! Of course not,' it said, rather offended. '*Flies!* That's what bats eat – flies!'

Doorkins looked slightly less anxious. It helped that the bat had a friendly squashed face with enormous sticky-up ears.

'Pippin's the name!' SNIFF. SNIFF. 'Is that manure?' Pippin asked, wrinkling her already very wrinkly nose.

'Yes, and what's it to you?' snapped Mole. She appeared to be getting fed up with the whole thing, which was most unlike her.

'Only asking,' said Pippin, a little wounded. 'Besides, we don't have a problem with manure. It attracts our supper.'

Mole looked a little embarrassed. 'Sorry,' she

said. 'I've just had enough of this lot.' She waved a paw at the bandits below.

'Tell me about it!' blurted the little bat. 'They've only gone and hijacked our home.'

'Really?' asked Weasel in shock.

'Yes, really! The whole tree and everything,' she blubbered. 'We've got nowhere to go. That's why we're buzzing around here in such a tizz.'

CLUNK! A round wooden door burst open and a rough-looking stoat with an eye patch leaned out.

'Hold it there, you good-for-nothings!' the stoat yelled harshly to the ferrets below. The net immediately came to a halt.

'That's Tarquin the jailer! I'm off!' said the little bat nervously and flapped away to join her friends.

The stoat leaned out and dragged the net towards the opening.

'Just 'ow many more of you is there gonna be?'

he said, pulling them roughly through the hole. 'We're running out of room 'ere. Good job we keep those batty bats locked out.'

Weasel had a bad feeling about this. Who, or what, did they have stashed inside this ginormous tree!?

'Phew-wee! What you lot been rollin' in?' The stoat cringed, pinching his snout.

'Ahem! Now look here, my good man,' Weasel began, though he didn't think this rogue was particularly good at all. 'Just let us go and we'll say no more about it.'

'Why? Do you 'ave somewhere to be?' Tarquin growled.

'Well, of course!' Weasel replied haughtily. 'We've got to be in New Pineland quick smart, and– OUCH!' Doorkins had elbowed him sharply in the ribs.

'Top secret, remember, Weasel! Top secret!' he whispered from behind his paw. Weasel covered his mouth quickly. In his sour mood, he'd almost given it all away.

'Well, you ain't going anywhere, my friend. Boss's orders!' said the jailer menacingly. He dragged them on to a big squashy platform, jumped to a nearby vine and slipped into the darkness below. Agent Mole wriggled to the edge to peer after him.

'Oh my goodness.' She quivered. 'Whatever you do, don't look down there!'

Mole did not like heights one bit. She was

happiest crawling around underground. Weasel, who just had to see, ignored Mole's warning and edged closer to peek over.

GULP!

They were extremely high up! He squinted his eyes into the dingy void. Far below, moonlight came in through the entranceway. He could see bandits busying around on the ground, doing bandity-type stuff. In the centre was a large pile of leaves and woodland debris.

'That must be the Highway Hedgehog's nest. Probably where she is having a nap this very moment,' Weasel said.

Doorkins shuffled over for a clearer view. Dormice thought nothing of scary heights; they were used to scampering about high trees anyway.

'Hmmm, plate fungi,' he said, prodding the soft spongy platform. Doorkins was an expert in all

growing plant things.

'Plate what?' asked Weasel.

All around the inside of the tree trunk were large dinner-plate-like mushrooms growing from the wall. But there was something sitting on top of each and every one.

'What *are* they?' Mole squinted.

'Th-they're animals!' exclaimed Doorkins.

Weasel stared at the mushroom below. 'No!' He gawped in shock. 'It can't be!' Lying on the nearest fungus, tied up and gagged, was H, the WI6 head-honcho hedgehog! What in squishy-bramble's name was going on!?

CHAPTER 11

A mean-looking brown rat stood guard over the WI6 boss. The dandy highway costume had gone, replaced by her usual plain work-like outfit.

'How can she be in two places at once?' puzzled Weasel. Both Doorkins and Mole looked baffled.

'There's something familiar about all these animals,' he said, stroking his chin. 'But I can't quite put my paw on it.'

'I'll tell you why they're all familiar,' blurted Doorkins. 'Because they're all WI6!'

Clattering cob nuts! Doorkins was right!

Now Weasel looked again, there were Boffin Bunnies, Special Branch sparrows, security badgers, decoy ducks, messenger pigeons … WI6 agents of all varieties. The bandits had nabbed the whole of Hedgequarters, which was the WI6 nerve centre! No wonder his spy hotline hadn't been ringing.

The super-spy felt his blood begin to boil.

UH-OH! The Weasel War Dance was coming on. And this time, he couldn't stop it. In a sudden frenzied effort to escape the net, he jiggled and twisted, arms swinging and legs kicking. But the more he did, the closer they slid towards the edge of the mushroom.

'Weasel! Snap out of it!' cried Mole. But Weasel couldn't hear. He thrashed around, dragging them nearer and nearer the edge. Until with a slow ... THWOP! ... over they went.

''Ere, what's goin' on?' called the rat guard, glancing up. The three friends dropped like a conker, flattening the rodent with a THWUMP!

'Well, I think that went rather well, don't you?' Weasel beamed, shaking the war dance mist from his noggin.

'UUUUGH!' groaned Mole and Doorkins. Mole would argue it was more luck than anything else, if she wasn't so frazzled from the fall.

A strange, strained mumble came from the back of the mushroom. 'UMMM. UMMM. UMMM ...'

'H!' cried Doorkins with worry.

'Hang on a minute!' said Mole. 'Wasn't she the one who put us in this net in the first place?'

H's eyes widened. She shook her head fiercely and the strangled mumbling continued.

'Let's see what she's got to say for herself,' suggested Weasel.

They shuffled over to the hog-tied hedgehog, which proved a little tricky, as they were still trapped in the net.

'OUCH!'

'EEK!'

'OI, WATCH MY TAIL!'

As they eventually reached the bound-up WI6 boss, Weasel reached out a paw and pulled down her gag.

'Blaaargh!' she croaked. 'It's about time you lot turned up! How dare you blame me for all this bother!? Get me untied and—'

Weasel pulled the gag back over her mouth.

'Phew, she has got a lot to say for herself,' said

Mole, raising her eyebrows.

'UMMM! UMMM! UMMM!' growled H, eyes wide and thrashing around.

'Calm down, H! Calm down,' soothed Doorkins. The little mouse could be quite good at calming others – not so much himself, though. As the head honcho gradually stopped jiggling, Weasel leaned in and pulled down the gag.

'Oh! What's that pong?' she said with a grimace. Mole immediately went to pull up the gag again. She'd just about had enough.

'N-no!' gasped H. 'It's m-my twin sister!'

'Who's your sister?' asked Weasel with a puzzled look.

'Who do you think? The Queen of England, of course!' barked the hedgehog grumpily.

'Er … I think she means the Highway Hedgehog,' whispered Mole.

'Well, I never!' gasped Weasel, genuinely quite surprised. His eyes narrowed in suspicion as he glanced at his friends, who also looked unsure.

'Look in my pocket, if you don't believe me!' she said, nodding to the top pocket of her jacket. With her paws tied, H had no chance of reaching it. Mole crawled forward, and reached in to pull out a small, folded picture. It showed two cute hedgehog hoglets in a hug.

'She's my evil twin,' sighed H.

Doorkins leaned over to look at the picture. 'She doesn't look very evil,' he said.

'No, she wasn't then,' said H a little sadly. 'But Henrietta's so jealous of how important I've become.'

The friends tried to hold in a giggle. *Henrietta.*

It didn't sound much like a fierce highway bandit. Now they couldn't help but wonder what 'H' stood for …

'It's Hortense, if you must know,' said H, as if reading their minds. All three held back an even bigger snigger and H frowned. 'ANYWAY! My sister is set on putting an end to me and WI6. Don't know why, really. She seems to be doing quite well with this whole bandit thing.'

Doorkins went to untie the WI6 boss through the holes in the net, when Weasel held him back.

He couldn't help but worry about their mission. They had promised Captain Barney-Barnster that they would get a message to the Fearless Animal Fire-Fighting Squadron, FAFFS for short.

'Hang on, buddy, we have to get to New Pineland, and the extra baggage … you know,' he said, flicking his eyes towards H. The hedgehog wasn't exactly built for speed; she might be safer left where she was.

'We can't just leave her!' Doorkins whispered.

'She'll be fine,' Weasel insisted before turning to H. 'H, I promise we'll be back to rescue you soon … ish,' he said, pulling her gag back up. The hedgehog writhed and wriggled in protest. *I'm never going to hear the end of this*, thought Weasel.

The friends dragged themselves to the edge of H's mushroom platform.

'It'll be a jolly old trick getting down there. We'll be seen for sure!' said Mole, gazing into the gaping hollow below. Then Weasel noticed the dangling creeper – the one the bandit stoat Tarquin had used. It seemed to go all the way to the ground; Weasel was sure he could just about reach it.

'GRRRRRR! If it wasn't for this wretched net,' he grumbled in frustration.

'Maybe we could jump for it ... together?' suggested Doorkins. Mole looked mightily uncertain – heights were not her thing.

Moments later, they had shuffled their way forward, to stand nervously on the edge of the plate mushroom. The gap between them and the vine seemed much wider now.

'After three, everybody,' said Weasel, a little unsure himself.

Then ... THWUMP-OOOF! Without warning, something small and solid hit Weasel, throwing him off balance and, as if in slow motion, he toppled into the others and knocked them flat.

CHAPTER 12

CHOMP! CHOMP! CHOMP!

Agent Weasel blinked open his eyes. What on earth was that noise?

'Don't worry, I'll get you out of here!' It was Pippin the little bat, nibbling away with her extra-sharp teeth.

'Er ... thanks for that!' said Doorkins, rubbing the rising lump on top of his head.

'How did you manage to get in here, Pippin?' asked Mole.

Pippin paused chomping to answer. 'It was that nincompoop, Tarquin.' CHOMP! CHOMP! CHOMP! 'He left the door open ...' CHOMP! CHOMP! CHOMP! 'And I snuck in!' CHOMP! CHOMP! SNAP! 'There, finished,' she said cheerily, as the net fell apart. Mole, Doorkins and Weasel gratefully wriggled out.

'Ahh, that feels good!' said Weasel, stretching. It felt like they'd been in there for yonks.

'Thanks, Pippin!' Doorkins said.

'Yeah, great job!' Mole added. And the little bat beamed proudly.

A loud, muffled grumbling caught their attention. It was H, still fuming at the back of her mushroom prison. You could almost see the steam jetting out of her ears! Weasel ignored this – the poor head honcho would have to wait – and turned back to his friends.

'I have an idea!' he declared.

Mole and Doorkins looked at each other doubtfully. They thought their friend was brilliant, but it was just that, sometimes, the super-spy's ideas could be a little … off-key. Weasel didn't notice the look that passed between his friends. He was too busy whispering something in Pippin's rather large and pointy ear. She nodded keenly – which was probably a good sign, they thought – her small face scrunched in concentration.

The plan was a rather simple one, but a plan all the same. Perched on the edge of the mushroom again, the trio waited.

'Now, Pippin!' cried Weasel. Suddenly, the door above burst open and hundreds of squealing bats shot through. They spiralled down into the hollow, creating a dark curtain. Making the perfect cover for the animals' escape!

H bucked and grumbled frantically. Weasel felt terrible for leaving her tied up, but they'd be back for her soon – he hoped!

Agent Weasel began to think his plan might actually work. With all this squeaky fluttering, the bandits surely wouldn't be able to see a thing.

'FOLLOW ME!' he yelled, and leapt for the creeper. As Weasel grabbed hold, he looked down to check his friends had made it. There was Mole, clinging on for dear life. But where was Doorkins?

'DOORKINS, DOORKINS!' he yelped in alarm. Weasel tried to spot his best pal, but with all the fluttering bats it was impossible!

'I'm here, Weasel!' squeaked an unmistakeable little voice. Weasel snapped his head round and there, hovering behind him, was Pippin gripping on to a rather embarrassed dormouse by the ears.

'All that flapping startled me and I panicked,' said Doorkins, with an apologetic shrug.

'Phew! As long as you're safe, good buddy,' Weasel gasped in relief.

Doorkins looked up at Pippin and smiled.

'At least I can say one thing ... that I officially like bats now.'

'This is all very well, but c-can we get down to the ground?' Mole quaked. The poor thing clung on to the creeper with her eyes tight shut.

The cloud of bats concealed the way whilst the friends shimmied towards the ground. Weasel grinned when he realised that the leathery little creatures were also taking their own revenge – by pooping on the pesky bandits! And, boy, were bats good at pooping! They showered the poor rogues as they dashed about in panic.

'The creeper's too short,' cried Mole desperately.

It was true. The animals dangled some way above the Highway Hedgehog's leaf pile. *Oh no*, thought Weasel, *we're going to have to drop!*

'Well, at least we'll have a soft landing,' he said,

eying the heap of leaves and twigs below.

'Oh great!' said Mole sarcastically. 'Though I suppose it's better than a pile of manure.'

'I'll go first!' Weasel called. He took a deep breath and tensed, ready to leap.

'Here I go then!' he bellowed, springing into the air. He threw his arms out into a star shape, much like a flying squirrel. He hoped to glide down gracefully, avoid crashing into Mole and Doorkins on the way, and land lightly on the leaf pile below. But Weasel's descent was anything but graceful.

Realising he wasn't actually a flying squirrel, Weasel lost his nerve midway. Instead of gliding, he plummeted down, hitting Mole and Doorkins on the way. Poor Pippin lost her grip on Doorkins, who, along with Mole, hurtled through the air. The three animals crashed, screaming all the way, through the nest's makeshift roof and right into the Highway Hedgehog's private chamber.

CHAPTER 13

Weasel scrabbled around in the dingy leaf pile, searching for his friends.

OUCH! He looked at his poor arm where he had pricked himself on something very sharp and spiky. GULP! It could only be one thing …

'WHO DARES DISTURB MY SLUMBER?' boomed the Highway Hedgehog. The WI6 spy nearly jumped out of his fur.

'Quick, this way,' Mole whispered right in his ear and Weasel nearly leapt out of his fur again before finding himself suddenly being dragged through wads of moss and leaves.

'She seems to know where she's going,' chirped Doorkins, who held on to her other spade-like paw.

They'd have been in a right pickle without Mole! She had a keen sense of smell and touch, making rooting around in the dark her specialty.

Suddenly, the animals were out of the nest and stumbling into a scene of utter mayhem. The bats zoomed around, poop-bombing the terrified bandits. The bandits screeched and squawked, trying to find cover but without much luck.

'Well, this is a jolly sight, isn't it?' said Weasel, taking in the view. Just as a big plop landed right on his head. AGAIN!

'Oi, on the bandits! Not us!' he yelled crossly, shaking the gloop from his fur.

'Sorry!' called an apologetic Pippin. She darted about just above their heads, looking a little wide-eyed and anxious. 'I'm having a bit of trouble controlling this lot!' She nodded to the dipping and diving bats above.

'Where are those little pests? I'll string 'em up by their toes if I catch them!' bellowed the bandit leader. Her yelling sounded like it was coming from the opposite side of the leaf pile. Even so, they certainly had no trouble hearing her.

'Maybe we should get out of here?' suggested Doorkins, glancing nervously at the bats.

'What an excellent idea, my friend,' replied Weasel. 'But the question is, how?' Weasel pointed to the large exit hole leading outside. A gaggle of quaking bandits sheltered there in an attempt to avoid the flying bat plop. There was no way through!

'I know a way!' said a voice behind them. The animals snapped round to see their old friend Nutter Bush-tail.

'You rotter!' growled Mole. 'You betrayed us! Your own friends!'

'I-I can explain,' blurted the little squirrel. 'Henrietta has all the WI6 agents hostage, including H. She threatened to dunk them in a toxic field ditch if I didn't do what she said. She wants her sister's job – proper jealous, she is.' Nutter looked incredibly sad and Weasel couldn't help but feel sorry for her. He still felt a little doolally himself after his dip in the ditch gloop; he didn't want any other animal to go through that.

'Find them now!' roared the Highway Hedgehog.

'I can help you, but you'll have to trust me,' said Nutter urgently.

'All right,' said Weasel, giving in. 'But no more net shenanigans, OK? That wasn't fun at all.'

The squirrel nodded eagerly and then led the way.

The animals scarpered after the WI6 rookie agent, dodging bat poo as they went.

The inside of the hollow tree towered above them as they made their way to a large, knotty root on the opposite side.

Weasel fell behind slightly while avoiding poop that seemed to be making a beeline for him. With his attention skyward, he didn't notice the figure standing nearby until it was too late. BOSH! He crashed to the floor, stars dancing in front of his eyes.

'Oi! W-wot you doin' out of your net?' croaked Tarquin, the rough-looking stoat. He sat on the ground opposite the WI6 spy, looking as woozy and confused as Weasel felt. In his distraction, Weasel had run RIGHT into the jailer.

'BOSS, THEY'RE OVER 'ERE!' yelled the stoat at the top of his lungs.

'Now, my dear fellow, let's not get overexcited,' hushed Weasel.

'BOSS! BOSS! BO—' SPLAT! The biggest bat plop Weasel had ever seen landed right on top of the stoat's head.

'Oi!' yelled the stoat. He looked up at the cloud of bats, shaking a fist. 'Oh, wait until I get my paws on you filthy bats!'

Weasel was enjoying the scene so much, he didn't realise he'd been spotted.

'THERE HE IS!' cried one of the ferrets by the leaf pile.

'I'd love to hang around, old chap, but I must be off. Nice meeting you again!' he said to the goo-coated stoat. Tarquin groaned wearily.

He looked around for his friends, but they were nowhere in sight. Where had everyone gone? No Doorkins, Mole or Nutter. Just a load of splattered bat poop and frantic bandits.

'PSSSSSSSST!' came a loud hiss.

OH, THANK THE GOOGLY GOOSE-GOGS, it was Nutter! She peeked out from behind a thick root near the inside wall of the tree, gesturing for him to hurry up. Weasel didn't need to be told twice!

'WHAT ARE YOU WAITING FOR? GET AFTER HIM, YOU COMPLETE HADDOCKS!' hollered the baddie hedgehog from some way behind.

This gave Weasel the jolt he needed. Sprinting as fast as he could, he leapt over the nearby root. But as he did, there was no Nutter Bush-tail on the other side. Only a deep, dark hole, which he plunged straight into ...

'YEEEEEEEOOOOW!'

CHAPTER 14

'Argh! Where in bloated bog-weed did he go?' fumed the prickly hedgehog bandit.

'D-don't know, boss, one minute he was there and the next—'

'Find him, NOW! Or else it'll be YOU disappearing next,' she screeched.

That hedgehog is going to do herself a mischief carrying on like that, thought Weasel. He lay face down at the bottom of the dark hole, completely unseen by the hunting baddies. Luckily, he had landed on soft, mulchy ground that had cushioned his landing.

'Come on, Weasel!' said Mole. 'This is no time for a nap.'

'Where are we?' asked the super-spy, standing up and dusting off his WI6 pullover.

'This is Worm Alley,' replied Nutter, leading the way. 'The secret back door out of Spooky Hollow. Even the Highway Hedgehog doesn't know about this secret passage!'

'Why is it called ...?' Weasel trailed off as he noticed Mole staring hungrily at the wriggly worms slithering out of the walls. Worms were her favourite nosh – as they were for most moles.

Gross! thought Weasel. He couldn't bear the

thought of a squidgy worm supper. Biscuits were more his thing. Any type, but particularly the round ones with a hole in the middle. And stripy icing on top, of course. Oh, what he'd do for a biscuit right now.

'Maybe we should get a move on?' suggested Doorkins, always the one to get them back on track. The bandits scrabbled about above, trying to work out how to get to them, but it wouldn't be long before they found the tunnel entrance.

'Anybody got a torch?' asked the little squirrel, squinting into the dark ahead.

'Of course, I always come prepared,' said Weasel, reaching for his WI6 survival rucksack.

But his rucksack wasn't there!

'Drat! It must've fallen off in the smash-up with that stoat.'

First the penknife, now the rucksack and ... OH

NO! His beloved copy of *The Big Bumper Book of Survival* was gone! Would he ever be able to whittle again? And he'd been so looking forward to making that coffee table.

Suddenly, a beam of light lit the way ahead. All the wriggly worms squirmed back into the darkness of the earth wall. Weasel realised then that the light wasn't coming from up ahead at all. It was coming from Mole's super-duper WI6 wristwatch. This watch had everything but the kitchen sink – and it probably had one of those as well! Weasel knew what would be top of his Christmas list this year.

'What's this 'ole doin' 'ere?' came a gruff voice from above.

'And there's a light!' added another.

Eek! The bandits had found the entrance.

'Switch off the torch,' whispered Nutter hastily. Mole did and they were plunged back into darkness!

They reached out for each other and grabbed paws, making a little crocodile chain. Mole used her super-keen senses to lead the way.

'Ugh … worms everywhere!' cried Doorkins. As soon as the torch went off, the wriggly creatures had crawled back out again! YUCK! Weasel felt a slimy body drag right across his face. *Worm Alley? More like Worm City!* he thought, a bit grossed out.

'GET DOWN THERE, YOU BIG BABIES!' bawled the bullying hedgehog.

'But, boss, it's dark! And it looks like the walls are … movin'!' whinged one of the minions.

'NOW!' she screeched. Weasel could just imagine the Highway Hedgehog shoving the bandits down the hole, one by one.

'UGH!'

'OH, 'OW 'ORRIBLE! I FEEL SOMETHING ON MY FUR!'

'OOH! YUCK!'

Obviously, the bandits had met the wiggly worms!

'No way these ruffians are catching us!' said Mole firmly. She instantly picked up the pace to a full-on gallop. But after a few strides, they screeched to a halt, bumping into each other.

'Uh! Left, or right?' asked Mole. There was a fork in the tunnel and Mole had no idea which way to go!

'I CAN 'EAR SOMEFING UP 'ERE,' said a gruff voice, getting closer.

'I have an idea. Quick, give me the watch!' said Nutter urgently. Mole instantly handed it over. *Well*, Weasel thought, *if I had known it was that easy, I would have asked for it ages ago!*

'You go left, I'll take the right,' said the squirrel. She switched the watch on to flashing mode and dashed off down the right-paw tunnel.

'FOLLOW THAT LIGHT!' yelled a voice, almost upon them. The bandit gang went dashing past. They didn't even notice the three animals taking cover in the shadows.

'Phew, that was close,' sighed Doorkins.

'I've changed my opinion on that young squirrel,' said Mole. 'She's a pretty top-drawer agent.' Coming from Mole, that meant a lot. Weasel just hoped his young apprentice would be OK. *Of course she will; she can handle anything.*

'What's that noise?' asked Doorkins, tweaking an ear worriedly.

A low rumbling sound shook the tunnel walls. The worms suddenly disappeared into the soil again. *What was going on?*

'BATS!' screeched the dormouse and belted off down the tunnel without a backwards glance, faster than Weasel had ever seen him go.

'WAIT, DOORKINS!' cried Weasel, but he was already gone. The thundering, high-pitched squeak of hundreds of bats got louder and louder. The tunnel shook around them and the ground vibrated beneath them.

'Right … let's not panic, Mole,' he said unconvincingly. They looked each other in the eye and … ran screaming in fright in the same direction as Doorkins!

CHAPTER 15

Weasel and Mole burst from the tunnel in a shower of earth and worms and rolled into a deep, dry ditch below.

And just in time too. The bats hurtled out overhead, screeching and flapping in a thunderous roar. They spiralled up into the night sky and back towards the top of the tree at Spooky Hollow.

'Sorry, friends. Must apologise for that lot,' said a voice from the grass verge above. It was Pippin; she clung to the stem of a giant hogweed that arched over the ditch.

'Aw! They're just happy to be back home, I'm sure,' said Weasel cheerily. 'Don't suppose you've seen our little dormouse anywhere, have you?'

'Up here, Weasel!' said Doorkins, dangling from the end of the hogweed plant.

As quick as lightning, the small bat was up and hovering next to her new dormouse friend.

'Grab on, Doorkins, I'll give you an airlift,' she cried, over the sound of her beating wings.

'Thanks, Pippin, you're the best,' said Doorkins, now safely on the ground. Pippin smiled and looked towards Spooky Hollow, where her family had just flapped off to.

'I can see you're keen to get back to your flock,' said Weasel to the little bat. 'But can I ask another favour?'

'Of course, Weasel,' Pippin said. 'Oh, and it's a cauldron, by the way.'

The woodland super-spy looked a little confused.

'That's what you call a group of bats,' she explained. 'A cauldron.'

'Well, I never! How very witchy!' he replied in surprise.

'What's the favour?' she asked.

'Would you mind nibbling those poor WI6 chaps free? You know, the ones back at the Hollow?'

'Even your uppity boss?' she queried, scrunching her little face.

'Hmmm! Good question,' he pondered. Mole nudged him and he added, 'I'm only kidding! Of course, H can be … difficult, but she's still head honcho.'

Weasel should have tried to sound more keen. Poor H, being cooped up all that time.

'It's as good as done,' she said, giving Doorkins and her new friends a little wave of her claw. 'Come and visit soon!' And she chirped off into the night air.

'Ah! I will, my dear bat … I will!' sighed the mouse, without realising he'd said it out loud.

'Don't like bats, eh?' said Weasel, giving his pal a little nudge.

'Ahem … Yes, well, I, erm …' he stuttered shyly.

Suddenly, a loud commotion came from further down the ditch.

'Hmmm! That sounds distinctly bandit-like to me,' said Mole with a frown.

They decided to investigate. Keeping to the dry grass on the verge above, the three animals sneaked along as quietly as they could.

Peering down into the ditch, Weasel could just make out a heap of squabbling figures.

'OI! OW! GET YOUR BUM OFF MY FACE!'

'SILENCE!' boomed the Highway Hedgehog. She stood in the exit of the second tunnel – the one Nutter had so bravely led the bandits down.

'Stop behaving like nincompoops and find those spies!' she spat. 'Once we have them, WI6 will be finished. And that goody-two-shoes sister of mine will be hog-tied for good and I will rule the United Woodlands for ever … MWAH-HA-HA-HA!'

There it was – the evil laugh. Weasel hadn't met a villain that didn't have one. But this heinous hedgehog had it completely wrong because soon, H would be free, along with all the other WI6 agents. And she didn't have a dangly-dingbat's chance of catching them.

'Weasel!' a voice unexpectedly whispered, right in his ear.

He shrieked, jumping ten feet in the air. 'Nutter, what are you doing? I would have pooped my pants, if I actually wore any!' He trembled. Nutter shrugged apologetically.

'HEY, IT'S THEM!' cried one of the bandits from down below, as they began to scramble up the bank.

'Quick, let's go!' said Weasel, looking round. But his friends had already scarpered.

'Oi! Wait for me,' he cried, dashing off through the grass, and back towards the Hedge Highway.

CHAPTER 16

'AW! Boss, I'm soooo tired! Can we stop for forty winks ... pleeeease?' whined a ferret somewhere at the back.

'FORTY? You can't even have ONE!' screeched the hedgehog leader. 'Bandits never get tired. NEVER EVER!'

'Hmph! Funny that bosses seem to get a nap whenever they want,' quipped a smirking water rat under his breath. Some of the other bandits sniggered but soon stopped when the Highway Hedgehog glared at them. She kicked an old hazelnut case angrily, which bounced off the ferret's nose and hit the rat in the forehead.

'Ow!'

Weasel could hear the bandits bickering some way back. Why couldn't these baddies just get on? You know, like they did at WI6. Then he remembered some of the tizzies he'd had with H. Maybe the two sisters were the problem! They were twins and pretty much hated each other. If only they'd make up, then maybe all this hoo-ha would be over, and Weasel and his friends could get back to their mission!

'H-how are we going to sh-shake these blinking ne'er-do-wells?' gasped Mole, jogging alongside Weasel, who didn't seem out of breath one bit. After all, he did come from a long line of champion woodland runners. 'They've been on our tails for ages now, and we've got a mission to complete.'

Nutter and Doorkins nodded in agreement. Doorkins could barely speak, his stubby little legs going ten to the dozen.

'If only we had my copy of *The Big Bumper Book of Survival*,' Weasel pondered out loud.

'Well, why didn't you say!' Mole beamed, grinding to a halt. Reaching into her WI6 survival rucksack, she pulled out her very own copy of *The Big Bumper Book of Survival*!

This book looked in much better condition than Weasel's copy. There was no sticky bun grime or dog-eared pages. Plus, when he thumbed through, rather than the usual whittling stuff, there were lots of useful survival tips and tricks he'd never seen before!

'This is amazing, Mole!' he said, open-mouthed.

'It's the second edition,' she replied proudly. 'Hardly any whittling at all.'

Hmmm! Weasel wasn't sure how he felt about that – he did love whittling! But how come Mole seemed to get all the latest stuff, anyway? He'd have to have a word when they got back to Hedgequarters.

Weasel fumbled up his WI6 spy pullover.

'If we're going to build a trap, we're going to need a …' He pulled something out.

'Plastic spoon?' said Nutter, confused.

'Well, my penknife has gone … and this is the best I can do.' Weasel shrugged matter-of-factly. 'Unless …'

He looked to Mole, who shook her head sadly. Maybe she didn't have everything after all.

'Ah! Let's get to work then,' he said with a sigh.

CHAPTER 17

With a suitable springy branch found, the trap was just about complete. Doorkins cocked an ear for any sign of approaching bandits.

'Squabbling at twelve o'clock,' he said with a slicing motion of his paw.

But surely it's the early hours of the morning – two or three, maybe, thought Weasel.

Ah! He'd fallen for it again! His mouse buddy

obviously meant the direction of twelve o'clock. He could now hear the bickering bandits not far off.

'Everybody in position,' he whispered, trying to remember where he was supposed to be.

'Don't forget, Weasel, once they see you, run as fast as you can,' hissed Mole. She crouched by the trap's trigger, which happened to be made from the plastic spoon – useful after all!

He was going to be the bait! This made him a little trembly, if he was perfectly honest, but he tried not to show it. His friends needed him.

'Remember, Her Highway Highness has to step into the noose and then I'll spring the trap,' said Mole with a thumbs-up.

Weasel gave her a small smile, looking a bit peaky.

Doorkins and Nutter hid in the undergrowth opposite Mole. His mouse buddy covered his eyes with his paws, which didn't exactly fill the super-spy with confidence.

'HOW-WUGA! HOW-WUGA!' called Nutter. That was the secret bird signal they'd agreed on – what kind of bird nobody knew, but in this case, it meant the bandits were coming!

Weasel stood smack-bang in the middle of the Hedge Highway, right in the path of the advancing outlaws.

'Of course I'm better than you at hopscotch!'

'Wot a load of tosh! You couldn't hop a scotch if you tried!'

'Is that right? I bet I could hop …' The bandit paused to glance around. '… that spy there! Oh— Boss, there's a spy there!'

'I can see that, you chump,' grumbled the Highway Hedgehog.

Weasel didn't feel it, but he posed bravely with his paws on his hips. 'What are you waiting for,

Halfwit Hedgehog!? Come and get me!'

But she just grinned slyly, waggling her eyebrows at him. Why wasn't she taking the bait? He'd have to up the stakes.

'STINKY BANDIT BOTTOM-BURPS! STINKY BANDIT BOTTOM-BURPS!' he chanted.

'GET HIM!' yelled the fuming scoundrels.

'STOP!' howled their leader. 'CAN'T YOU SEE IT'S A TRAP?'

But her foolhardy mob were out of control! They raced forward, snarling and spitting viciously. Weasel wasn't hanging around – he turned and ran for it. But no sooner had he done so than a snail crawled across his path. WHACK! He kicked it! Accidentally, of course.

'EEEEEEE!' The poor creature gave a high-pitched squeal, darting into its shell for cover.

It sailed through the air and whacked Mole right in the eye!

'OH!' cried Agent Mole and, in her surprise, she accidently tapped the plastic spoon and released the branch.

I have a bad feeling about this, thought Weasel. And he was right. The noose tightened round HIS ankle and with a sharp THWIP! he flew into the air and the world tilted beneath him!

Every good agent knows that traps can be tricky things and, sometimes, they can go a little wrong. But let me tell you, this one went completely pear-shaped!

They'd made a classic trap-making beginner's error and selected an extra-springy branch.

It launched our woodland super-spy into the air and flung him about like a ragdoll. He boinged left, right and centre, and with a loud THWACK! he knocked the two bickering bandits out cold! The poor things didn't know what had hit them! Other than a WI6 weasel strapped to a springy branch, of course.

'Ha ha! It's like WHACK-A-MOLE but with bandits! No offence, Mole!' cried Nutter with a great big beaming grin.

'None taken,' she replied, her mouth agape, a hand pressed against her sore eye. This had not been the plan at all, but Weasel seemed to be doing a grand job biffing up these ruffians. Once he'd bounced to a halt, the bandits lay all around like flattened bowling skittles.

'Well done, old chap,' said Mole, sauntering up to the dangling super-spy. But Weasel was out for the count.

'Wait, I have just the thing!' said the little squirrel, pulling a small green bottle from her bag. They could just about make out the words 'Badger Poo' scrawled on the label.

'Ugh!' Doorkins cringed. 'Is that real badger poo?'

'Nooo, of course not! Just essence of badger poo,' replied Nutter.

'Oh! Well, that's all right then.' The dormouse shrugged.

One sniff of this stuff, and Weasel would be more awake than he'd ever been!

The friends untied his leg, lowering him gently to the ground.

'N-no, Granny, not the bath … I had one l-last year,' he mumbled in his dazed state.

Nutter swished the open bottle under Weasel's snout and the result was instant. His eyes bulged open and he leapt into the air, with a yell.

'WOW! Badger poo?' asked Weasel, his nostrils flared and eyes wide as millponds.

'Only the best,' answered Nutter with a cheeky wink. After he'd calmed down a bit, Weasel took in the scene.

'Well, that worked a treat, didn't it?' he said, looking round at the flattened bandits. 'But where's the bad-tempered hedgehog?'

'Eh?' puzzled Mole. They frantically searched – under, in and behind everything … but it was too late.

The Highway Hedgehog had vanished!

CHAPTER 18

Weasel licked his lips as the team jogged up the Hedge Highway. He thought of the delicious nettle pancakes he'd just scoffed for breakfast. Doorkins, a talented chef – amongst many other things – had quickly whipped up a recipe using Mole's book. It was just the energy boost Weasel had needed. Mind you, his mouth did feel a little numb and tingly, which is probably why no one else was tempted to eat them.

'Can't be berry bar m-now-th,' he slurred, the words coming out all wrong.

'Er … yes,' said Mole, relieved she hadn't eaten the pancakes. She studied her super-duper WI6 explorer map. 'Only a few stretches of hedge and we'll be in New Pineland!'

'Nice-th … map, by the wayzzz,' slobbered Weasel admiringly. Nutter handed the dribbling super-spy a drink of water. He guzzled it down eagerly.

'Ahh! Thunks, that's much butter,' he said with a slightly lopsided smile.

Earlier, the animals had scarpered, leaving the knocked-out bandits snoozing under the hedge. But no sign of that despicable hedgehog! Had she scarpered too?

A warm glow of light appeared on the horizon.

'Well, at least dawn's on the way,' said Doorkins thankfully.

'Ooh! Dawn from Best Bakes in Little Thicket? Is

she bringing biscuits?' asked Weasel excitedly.

'Ahh!' sighed the small mouse. The badger poo had brought Weasel round, but he was still a little doolally from the bandit-bashing. 'No, not that Dawn—' The dormouse paused mid-sentence and began to sniff the air. SNIFF, SNIFF.

'What's up, Doorkins?' asked Nutter worriedly. A sniff from the little mouse usually meant trouble!

'Hmmm! Something strange, but I can't quite put my paw on it,' he pondered, scratching his chin.

'I'm sure it's— Ouch!' Weasel tripped, nearly falling flat on his face. 'What in BUSHY BOBTAIL'S NAME was that?'

It was a sizeable red tin, bigger than Doorkins, with a large dent in the middle. 'DR POP'S BEST FIZZY SWIG', it read on the side.

'Look, there's stuff all over the place!' cried Nutter in horror. And she wasn't joking. As far as the eye could see, there were packets and wrappers, crumpled newspaper, half-eaten sandwiches and banana peels! There was even a manky glove and a giant boot with no laces and a VERY, VERY PINK SOCK!

'HUMANS!' said Mole with an angry tremble. Sometimes the big upright creatures could be so thoughtless, dropping their litter wherever they went.

'L-look!' said Doorkins, pointing a shaky paw.

They all gaped. Where the hedge should have been was a massive gap! And cutting right through were two sets of tyre tracks, as wide and deep as a ditch. Whatever had created it must have been extremely heavy. The soil was churned up and all the pretty wildflowers lay scattered and crushed. Suddenly …

DUH-DUM! DUH-DUM! DUH-DUM! DUH-DUM-DUH-DUM!

The animals dived for cover, expecting some kind of terrifying machine-thingy that could tear the countryside to bits.

'Oh, hello,' said a dozy voice from somewhere high above. Weasel slowly looked up to see a large hoof planted just inches from his head! 'Are you havin' a nap?' the voice asked.

Weasel and the others carefully got to their paws.

The animal moved closer, sniffing Weasel with a large, wet nose.

'No, we were, er … inspecting the grass,' he replied, looking up. Weasel could see now that it wasn't a machine-thingy at all, but a giant red deer!

'You don't look much like grass inspectors to me,' said the deer, like he'd actually met one before. 'I'm Brian, by the way.'

'Hello, Brian. I'm Agent Weasel and these are my friends. We're on a very important mission,' explained Weasel proudly.

'Well, I'm a bit lost,' said Brian. He was only a young fawn and at that age, they would normally travel with a herd, but there wasn't another deer in sight.

'Where do you live, young fella-me-lad?' asked Mole, in a kind voice.

'Oh! New Pineland!' he said, as though in a dream. 'But I can't find it.'

'Well, you're in luck!' chirped Mole. 'That's exactly where we're off to!'

Brian brightened. 'Really? Can I come with you?'

'Of course! The more the merrier,' boomed Weasel, patting the deer on the hoof. Who could say no to those big, doe-y brown eyes?

They marched along the Hedge Highway with Brian plodding along on the grass verge. He stopped every now and again, worriedly sniffing bits of the scattered litter.

'Hmmm,' murmured Mole, squinting at the map. 'Something's not quite right ...'

'Problem, Mole?' asked Weasel, wondering if the map wasn't quite as super-duper as he'd imagined.

'It's just that, according to my map, New Pineland should be right here!'

Mole walked ahead a few steps. 'Oh no!' The others hurried over to see what was wrong.

Before the animals lay a low, scrubby hillside. And as far as the eye could see, there were hundreds upon hundreds of tree stumps.

'What's this?' said Nutter, crouching by an old log sign on the ground. The little squirrel brushed away the pine needles and read, 'N-New Pineland!'

Everybody gasped. What had happened? The woodland was gone? There was a loud whimper and Brian bolted across the field.

'M-M-MUMMY!' he cried.

CHAPTER 19

'Poor kid wants his mummy,' said Weasel, shaking his head sadly. 'It must be too much seeing his home like this.'

'No, look! It actually is his mummy!' said Doorkins, pointing a paw across the field.

An adult deer stood by an open gate and Brian bounded up to her. The doe nuzzled his neck, turned, and the pair trotted off into the meadow beyond, their fluffy white bums bobbing as they went. The young fawn looked back for a moment and gave the friends a wide beaming smile.

'Aw, well, at least Brian got his happy ending,' said Mole. 'But what are we going to do about all this?' She waved her big paws at the ruined woodland.

The animals wandered into the strange landscape. Never had Weasel seen anything like it. Yes, Farmer Garrett would chop down the odd tree, but he would always plant another in its place. And even he would never, ever leave a horrible mess like this!

'Don't suppose we'll find any fire experts now,' Weasel sighed gloomily.

'Where do you suppose all the animals went?' asked Doorkins, looking hopefully behind a tree stump.

'WHERE INDEED!?' said a familiar haughty voice.

The startled friends spun round. There, perched on a rock shaped a bit like a cow's bottom, stood the Highway Hedgehog, paws on hips with her minions around her.

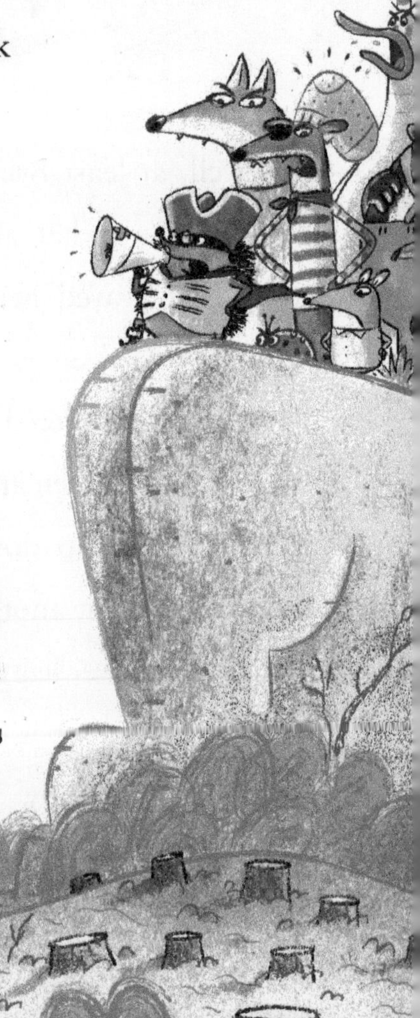

'Nice to see you again,' said Weasel, thinking it was not that nice at all.

'Did you know all of this was once mine?' she sneered, waving her arms at the scruffy hillock.

Tarquin coughed pointedly. Weasel was surprised to see that the stoat wore the pink sock they'd seen earlier on his head as a rather jaunty hat!

'I mean, er ... ours,' the Highway Hedgehog corrected.

'You mean you actually lived here?' said Nutter in shock.

'Yes, it was much nicer then, of course, my little double-crossing friend,' she replied, glaring fiercely at Nutter. Nutter shrugged.

'I was Head Hedgehog ... and these lot' – she gave a sideways nod to the bandits – 'were my students.' Her gang nodded in agreement, though some still looked a little woozy from the earlier bashing.

Well, blow me down with a pheasant's tail feather, thought Weasel. That's why they'd turned to a life of crime on the Hedge Highway: the poor scoundrels had lost their home twice!

'And now thanks to you pesky spies, we've been turfed out of Spooky Hollow too,' she said, as if reading Weasel's mind. 'Well, you're not going to get away with it. I have a plan for you lot!'

'Just try it, you overgrown pin cushion!' barked Agent Mole, crouching into a fighting stance with her paws up. The others followed her lead and did the same – even Doorkins, who held up his little leather bag, ready to thwack any approaching hoodlums.

But the Highway Hedgehog gave a wide, unsettling grin. Only then did Weasel notice that she was spinning the end of a rope in her paw.

'Uh-oh!'

Without warning, she gave it a sudden tug. There was a loud THWIP! WHOOSH! and up they went, finding themselves squashed together in another net. The four friends dangled from a weak, bendy tree sapling. Probably the only one left in such a lifeless place.

'You're rather good at these traps,' said Weasel. 'Maybe you could give us some tips one day; ours don't seem to work too well. And in exchange, we have a good soap recipe for bat poo stink.'

The bandits grumbled, no doubt remembering the incident with the little leathery creatures.

'Smelly bat poo will be the least of your worries,' said the Highway Hedgehog. 'Just wait and see what we've got in store for you.'

CHAPTER 20

Without any trees to shade them, the sun beat down on the friends.

'Looks like it's going to be another scorcher,' said Doorkins, fanning himself with his mousey ears.

'I believe so, my friend,' agreed Weasel. 'Just wish I had my swimming costume on!'

The bandits roughly strapped the four friends to an enormous log pile the humans had made.

'OUCH!' Weasel complained as a hazelnut hit him right in his noggin. It was that ruffian stoat, Tarquin, still wearing the very pink sock for a hat.

'Oi, watch it!' the super-spy yelled, rubbing his forehead painfully.

'Now that we have your attention,' called the Highway Hedgehog from below, 'I have an important speech to make.'

She had a funnel-shaped loudhailer, made from newspaper and bits of rubbish, which somehow made her voice boom even louder than usual.

'The humans will soon be back to take away what is left of our home,' she began, pointing at the large stack of pine logs the friends were tethered to. 'And when they load up their giant monster trucks,' she said, narrowing her eyes, 'you'll all be squished flat as pancakes at the bottom of a ginormous pile! MWU-HA-HA-HA-HA!'

'Did someone say pancakes?' Mole, totally bored with the Highway Hedgehog's speech, had drifted off. But one mention of tasty grub and she was wide awake again.

The Highway Hedgehog chose to ignore her.

'You don't understand,' Doorkins barked crossly. 'We have a mission to complete!'

Weasel and Nutter nodded in agreement.

'Someone has been starting fires in the United Woodlands and they're getting out of control. We came here to find firefighting experts to help us put a stop to it!'

'Ah yes, woodland does catch fire very easily,' the Highway Hedgehog continued smugly. 'These experts you've been looking for, they wouldn't happen to be the Fearless Animal Fire-Fighting Squadron, FAFFS for short?'

She held out her paws, gesturing to her crew.

No! These ragged ruffians couldn't possibly be the infamous fire experts they had been searching for! thought Weasel.

The Highway Hedgehog smiled gleefully. 'Yes, we pride ourselves on our fire-putting-out expertise, but more recently, we've learnt a thing or two about starting them!' The hedgehog held up a large yellow box.

Weasel squinted.

Dr Pop's Best Safety Matches.

GULP! The picture on the front showed a collection of little sticks with a red bobble on the end; he'd seen them before. Humans used the things for starting bonfires, barbecues and even fireworks!

'Those odd little fires in United Woodlands recently,' she continued, raising her eyebrows menacingly. 'Well, that was our teeny-weeny practice run. Now we're ready for the big one!'

'Why, you rotten ruffians!' cried Nutter.

'Starting fires is against the Countryside Code!' squeaked Doorkins angrily.

'You think we care about the Countryside Code?' growled Tarquin the stoat. 'We lost our home! We're bandits now and we fear absolutely nothing!'

'Yeah!' said Ferret One. 'Why should you keep your home when we lost ours, eh?'

'Doesn't sound very fair to me!' his ferret pal agreed.

'You won't get away with this!' yelled Mole.

'We'll bring the United Woodlands to its knees and that snooty sister of mine won't be so smug then. Anyway, who's going to stop us?' the Highway Hedgehog asked, waggling a paw in their general direction. 'You definitely won't be able to, BECAUSE YOU'LL BE COMPLETELY AND UTTERLY SQUISHED! MWU-HA-HA-HA-HA!'

And with that, the gang turned and trotted off on to the Hedge Highway, heading directly for the United Woodlands!

'What a pickle!' declared Nutter.

'A pickle?' bellowed Mole. 'It's a bit more than a pickle, Nutter! They're going to burn down our woodland home!'

VRUUUUM! VRUUUUM! The sound echoed down the lane and vibrated through the logs.

'Oh golly,' Mole whispered. 'The human trucks … they're here …'

As the trucks got closer, the noise got louder and louder, until a giant green monstrosity trundled over the hill. It had eight massive tyres and a humongous metal arm. On the end of the arm hung a great yellow claw!

‘Th-the humans are coming to s-squish us.’ Doorkins shuddered as the contraption thundered towards them.

‘Wait! I have something in my bag that might just help,’ said Nutter calmly. ‘I can’t reach it! Weasel, can you just …?’

Weasel twisted until he was able to stretch a paw into the little squirrel’s satchel. Suddenly, he clasped on to something familiar.

CLANK

'Is that …? MY WI6 SURVIVAL PENKNIFE!' he exclaimed.

'I found it on the floor near the hedgehog's leaf pile,' said the young woodland spy. 'It's covered in bat poo, but still ready to whittle!'

The log pile shook as the terrifying machine got nearer.

'QUICK, WEASEL, GET CUTTING!' cried Mole urgently. The super-spy fiddled the penknife behind his back and, in excited desperation, proceeded to fumble and drop it through the woodpile. CLATTER! CLATTER! CLICK! CLACK! CLICK!

'Oh, thank goodness, Nutter! With that knife, we'll be out of this in a jiffy,' said Mole in relief. 'How's it all going, Weasel?'

'Er, well …'

The massive machine rolled closer and closer.

CHAPTER 21

'What do you mean, you DROPPED it?' screeched Mole. Weasel glanced shamefully at his WI6 colleague.

He hadn't meant to! The bat poo had made it surprisingly slippery.

The incredibly noisy and terrifying contraption

moved in close enough that Weasel could see its driver in the front cab: a thin, balding man guzzling a steaming drink from a large cup while steering the machine with one hand. When he finished slurping, he belched loud enough that they could hear it over the engine and threw the cup carelessly from his window.

'The cheek!' squeaked Doorkins angrily.

What was it with these humans? You didn't see animals going around dropping rubbish in towns, did you? Well, maybe the odd little plop here and there ... but still!

As the vehicle pulled up, a big cloud of black smoke puffed from its exhaust. The animals coughed and choked; the burnt, sour smell was unbearable and made their eyes water.

'We've ... *cough!* ... got to ... *cough!* ... get out of here!' spluttered Mole. But it was too late. The machine's gigantic arm hovered over the trembling log pile.

'It's been an honour to serve alongside you, Agent Weasel,' said Nutter to her hero spymaster.

'Likewise, Agent Bush-tail,' Weasel replied sadly. He wasn't one for giving up easily, but there was just no way out of this mess. The huge metal claw clamped down on some logs above, making the friends cry out in fear.

'I think I've just done a bit of wee!' yelled Doorkins, over the loud scraping noise.

'You and me both, little buddy!' admitted Weasel to his best chum. The claw came down again and the poor animals were lifted into the air. They closed their eyes and held paws.

Then he felt a little flutter next to his ear and opened one eye to take a peek.

'MURIEL!' he cried. The tiny homing moth

perched on his shoulder, beaming away. *What is she doing here?* he thought.

'TALLY-HO, DON'T YOU KNOW!' came a sudden call from above. A pair of fierce talons slashed along the top of the log, cutting through the ropes like butter.

The friends screeched as they dropped loose and plunged towards the ground.

THUMP!

Weasel opened his eyes to find himself whooshing through the clear morning air on a feathery back,

Muriel still clinging to his shoulder.

'You OK up there?' asked a rather plummy squawk. Weasel let out a small whimper, unable to find his voice. 'Beaky Knock-Knock's the name,' the voice continued. 'Green Woodpecker Flying Squadron. Glad to have you on board.'

'P-pleased to meet you too,' the super-spy managed to blurt out, a little stunned.

'Can you imagine if someone took a picture of this?' Beaky laughed. 'A weasel on a woodpecker's back – it'd be all over the papers!'

'Er ... well, if you say so,' he replied uncertainly.

'Weasel, young fella! Good to see you in one piece, don't you know?' Captain Barney-Barnster appeared alongside them. A rather peaky-looking Agent Mole clung on to his back tightly.

Another beefy owl, who was carrying Nutter, glided in close by. The bird gave a little salute with the tip of its wing.

'This is Flying Officer O'Tawny; he doesn't say much. And, of course, you've met Wing Commander Beaky, don't you know?'

Weasel saluted back.

But hang on, somebody was missing.

'Oh Doorkins, not again!' Weasel looked around frantically for his best chum. He did have the habit of going missing at the most awkward of times.

'Here, Weasel,' squeaked a voice from below.

'Pippin!' he cried in relief. It continued to amaze Weasel how easily Pippin carried the rather frazzled-looking dormouse, who was nearly as big as she was. The little bat certainly had some bottle.

'Hello, friend! The whole family's tagged along!' She winked, nodding back to a cloud of bats dipping and diving frantically as one.

'If it wasn't for that little moth, you lot would be smushed by now,' said Commander Beaky.

'Yes, she's a proper trooper.' Weasel nodded, stroking Muriel's tiny head. She nuzzled his cheek affectionately.

'We should get back to the Woodlands pronto,' mumbled Agent Mole, her head buried in the owl's feathers. Heights were really not her thing!

'What's the rush, don't you know?' asked the Owl Force 1 captain. 'Shouldn't we look for this Fearless Animal Fire-Fighting Squadron while we're 'ere?'

'Old friend, we have a LOT to tell you!' Weasel said and, as they headed for their home, he explained the Highway Hedgehog's despicable deeds and the plan to burn the United Woodlands to a crisp.

'Knock me down with a dock leaf,' exclaimed the shocked barn owl. 'And H having a twin sister too, who'd have thought! Well, I've got to see this, don't you know?'

The barn owl banked a sharp left and rocketed downwards, flying just inches above the hedge top. Commander Beaky, Flight Officer O'Tawny and Pippin, with her batty entourage, followed close behind.

'YIPPEEEEEEE!' squealed Weasel in delight.

'Oh my giddy aunt!' moaned Mole, tightly shutting her eyes and holding on for all she was worth.

CHAPTER 22

They zoomed over Spooky Hollow, which looked totally deserted. And no wonder: all the batty bats fluttered behind them and the WI6 lot had been set free. Pippin assured Weasel that as soon as their ropes had been nibbled through, the animals had headed back to the United Woodlands. Weasel thought of H. She would give him a right ear-bashing for not untying her. In some way, he wished she'd stayed tied up if it meant avoiding that!

'Garrett's Farm dead ahead,' called Commander Knock-Knock.

They'd reached the farm in no time at all! This

journey was certainly much quicker by bird. If only the Boffin Bunnies could invent a set of WI6 wings, Weasel would get stuff done in a jiffy. Well, there was no harm in asking when next in Hedgequarters. *I really hope Hedgequarters isn't a pile of ashes by now*, he thought.

'Mrs Fluffykins at two o'clock, don't you know?' crackled Captain Barney-Barnster over Beaky's radio headset. Weasel was learning that this did not mean a two o'clock appointment with Mrs Fluffykins, but the direction he needed to look in. And when he did look, Weasel got one of the biggest shocks of his life!

'MEEEOW!' howled the vicious kitty from the roof of the dog kennel. She arched her back and hissed in anger, looking straight at Weasel. Fluffykins had sniffed the super-spy a long way off and wanted her revenge ... GULP!

'Let's give this puffed-up moggie a bit of a flyby,

don't you know?' chuckled the big, beefy barn owl. Barney-Barnster pulled down his goggles and got ready to dive.

'Are you s-s-sure this is a good idea, Capt—AAARGH!' screeched Mole as they plunged towards the farmyard. The WI6 agent gripped on with her powerful spade-like paws for dear life.

Mrs Fluffykins saw her chance and leapt into the air, swiping for the large owl. He swerved to avoid the sharp claws and zoomed straight into Garrett's barn. Fortunately, not the one the tractor had crashed into – there wasn't much left of that.

CLUCK-CLUCK! OINK-OINK! CRASH! SMASH! BASH! WALLOP!

Pippin and the bats immediately swooped down on the cruel kitty.

'YEEEOW!' she bawled as the small creatures surrounded her.

Weasel, Beaky and O'Tawny landed on the opposite end of the roof.

'I'll be s-s-s-seeing you later, Weasel,' Mrs Fluffykins spat fiercely, giving him the evils.

'Not if I see you first,' he called back.

This time, she was way too busy lashing out at the bats to respond. But the little creatures were far too quick and whenever she got close, they would just

fly out of reach. In her frustration, she teetered even further on the edge of the doghouse roof and …

'YEEEOW!' SPLOSH! Back into the old tin water trough she went.

There was a sudden cry from the United Woodlands, much louder than Mrs Fluffykins's yowls. Weasel squinted; there was smoke rising above the trees!

'FIRE!' squawked Commander Beaky.

'As much as I'd like to stay and help this poor kitty, it's time we were off,' said Weasel, nodding towards home.

Fluffykins thrashed around, spilling water on to Oi, who had slept through the entire thing but was now barking in irritation. This only set off Granny Garrett's pet magpie and Weasel's old enemy, the Robber King, who began to 'SQUAWK-CHAT-CHAT-CHAT!'

WHOOSH! BANG! went the farmhouse door. There stood Farmer Garrett, not looking best pleased, with half his breakfast down his shirt front.

The animals didn't hang about, quickly zooming off into the morning air. The woodland spy looked back as a puzzled Farmer Garrett fished the kitty from the water. Fluffykins scowled menacingly straight at Weasel. *Hmmm, not sure if I've quite made a friend for life there!* he thought.

'That looks like the rest of the WI6 guys,' said Beaky, pointing down towards the rather ditchy ditch. The same one Weasel had fallen into the other night. A group of animals scurried urgently over the bridge, making their way into the United Woodlands.

'That lot must be shattered; they'll have been scampering non-stop don't you know?' said Captain Barney-Barnster, no worse for his crash in the barn.

A bright orange glow appeared on the horizon.

And the gang could tell straight away that it wasn't the glow from the early morning sun. No, this was the glow of fire, a big fire – with lots of smoke, which you do tend to get with a fire.

'It's surrounded Little Thicket!' chirped Doorkins. He was right; the Highway Hedgehog had only gone and done it! What was she thinking? If she wanted to rule the Woodlands, there wasn't going to be much of it left! A ring of fire burned all around the outer edges of the village.

As they whooshed in, Weasel made out the Beefy Badger Brigade. They bounced on their big bottoms, trying to put out the blaze. But the fire was just too big!

The bandits were gathered on the village green, looking a bit twitchy and afraid. And no wonder! In front of them stood a lone figure, hurling what appeared to be a fearsome weapon above their head.

Who is this brave and powerful warrior? he thought.

As they neared, he could just make out …

'GRANNY!' cried Weasel.

His bold granny was facing down the whole gang of bullies … with just her handbag!

CHAPTER 23

'Come on, then, I'll take you all on!' cried Granny Weasel. She swung her handbag over her head, ready to swat a few bandit cronies.

She must be having a touch of the Weasel War Dance, thought Weasel as they landed behind her. It applied to all weasels, not just our super-spy hero.

'Granny, calm down,' cooed Weasel gently, making sure not to creep up on her for fear of being whacked himself.

'Ah! It's oojamaflip – 'bout time you showed up, boy!' she replied, still gunning for the bandits.

'You'd better get this old biddy out of here before she gets bashed!' growled Tarquin. His words were menacing but it was hard to take him seriously when he still had that pink sock on his head.

'HA!' scoffed Granny Weasel. 'You and whose army?'

'That would be me and MY army,' said the Highway Hedgehog, pushing through her minions to the front. 'GET THEM!'

'HENRIETTA!' called a loud, haughty voice

that Weasel was unfortunately very familiar with.

H stepped in front of Granny Weasel, face to face with her twin sister. The rest of the WI6 crowd gathered in behind them.

'Hortense,' said the bandit leader, using her sister's real name. This caused a few sniggers from the WI6 lot, which was quickly silenced with one look from the head honcho.

'Good to see you, sis, it's been too long,' she continued, with a slight sneer that suggested it actually hadn't been nearly long enough.

'Cut the nice talk, Henrietta,' grumbled H. 'Let's settle this like the old days, shall we?'

The Highway Hedgehog raised an eyebrow. 'Really? You want to wrestle?'

'Wrestle?' blurted Weasel in surprise. 'Aren't you both a little, er, too old for that?'

The twin sisters gave him a double hedgehog

stare, sending shivers right down his tail.

'Paw wrestle! Table and stools now!' the Highway Hedgehog demanded, and a table and two stools immediately appeared. H and her sister sat down and got ready to rumble.

'Is this really happening?' Weasel gawped.

'Looks like it,' said Doorkins excitedly. 'I'll have five acorns on the baddie!'

'Doorkins! How could you!?' Weasel replied in shock. He thought for a moment and quietly added,

'Actually, I'll put eight on the boss.'

Soon, there was a complete hullabaloo as everyone placed their bets and the acorns piled high.

'Er, excuse me! A little help over here?' It was Firefighter Babs of the Beefy Badger Brigade. The poor thing was bouncing uncontrollably. The crowd of animals just stared silently for a second and then, deciding that the badgers had everything under control, they turned back to the arm-wrestle match.

'HOW RUDE!' fumed Babs.

Agent Mole took on the role of referee.

'We want a clean, fair game, all right, ladies? Shake.' The two hedgehogs, serious as anything, bumped fists and glared each other down before clasping paws. 'Three ... two ... one ... WRESTLE!' Mole called.

A roar went up and the sisters strained for all they were worth! NAAAAAAAR! They swayed this way and then that way, over and over again before they locked in the middle. Sweat appeared on the sisters' brows, their eyes narrowed in utter focus.

The other animals cheered along at every twist and turn. Nobody noticed the poor badgers struggling with the flames.

Suddenly, the crowd went wild as H pushed her sister's paw to the table, then ... CLACKERTY-CLACK-CLACK!

Something fell from H's pocket. The Highway Hedgehog picked it up and ... smiled! Yes, *actually* smiled.

It was an oval frame that held a picture of two cute little hedgehogs. Young, happy and fresh as daisies.

The Highway Hedgehog stopped wrestling and reached for a necklace that hung around her neck. She opened a small clasp to reveal ... the same photo!

There was a collective 'Aww!' from the crowd.

'We were very close then,' said the Highway Hedgehog, a little sadly. 'Sometimes I wish we could be that close again.'

'Well, maybe if you stop being a ghastly baddie!' blurted H.

'Or maybe if you stop being a bossy-pants!' returned her sister. They growled at each other, standing sharply and slamming their paws on the table. Then the Highway Hedgehog's frown gradually turned to a twinkly grin.

'Hedgehog hug?' she asked gently, holding her arms out.

H's face softened. 'Hedgehog hug,' she said. And the two sisters embraced.

'Aww!' cooed the other animals.

'Oi! What about this arm wrestle? I've got a lot of acorns on this!' called a ferret from the back of the crowd.

'Never mind your silly acorns!' boomed Babs. She was still bouncing frantically on a patch of blazing grass. 'The fire is getting bigger!'

Everybody looked aghast. Babs was right! While they were distracted, the wind had picked up. And if you know anything about fires, you know fire and wind are a dangerous pair!

'The United Woodlands is doomed, I tell you! DOOMED!' cried Granny Weasel.

CHAPTER 24

'MORE WALNUTS, MORE WALNUTS!' ordered Henrietta the Highway Hedgehog.

'Who's being bossy now?' mumbled H under her breath. Henrietta chose to ignore this.

The New Pineland lot, being firefighting experts, had had the clever idea of using big walnut shells as buckets.

'Form a line, quickly!' Henrietta called, choosing

to ignore her sister's mumblings.

The row of animals went from Babble Brook to Little Thicket; those at one end used the shells to scoop up water and then passed it along the line. Those at the other end hurled it on to the fiery blaze. They did this again and again. Scoop, pass, splash! Scoop, pass, splash!

'IT'S JUST NOT ENOUGH!' cried Firefighter Babs. Her poor bottom was badly singed, but the brave badger kept on bouncing.

SPLASH

'WATCH OUT BELOW, DON'T YOU KNOW!' warned Barney-Barnster.

Water-filled party balloons soared through the air, landing with multiple sploshes! Even Muriel filled her little cheeks with water, spouting it over the raging fire. But nothing seemed to work.

The only animal who wasn't helping was … Agent Weasel!

He stood in the middle of the village green, swaying and waving his arms in the oddest way, making a strange siren noise!

'Well, I always knew this would happen,' H said to Mole. 'He's only gone and completely lost his marbles.'

Mole scowled at the WI6 boss. This was Agent Weasel; he would never let them down! *Though he is acting a little stranger than usual*, thought Mole.

Suddenly, a loud rumble filled the air. BOOOOOOOOOOM! The poor bats began to flap around in a wild panic, covering their ears and squeaking in terror. Everyone else dived to the ground except for Weasel, who carried on with his wild performance.

'What in bloomin' bally high was that?' Mole trembled as a big wet splotch landed on her nose. Tarquin felt it too and the big bad stoat's eyes widened with fear.

'BAT POO!' he cried. The last poop ordeal had been bad enough. They couldn't go through it again! The bandits panicked along with the bats, running around in circles. It was absolute chaos!

'It's not bat poo!' Mole yelled. She looked up at

the clouds in wonder. 'It's raindrops!'

Massive dark clouds drifted over to block the hot morning sun. And then it began to rain. And, oh boy, did it rain!

CHAPTER 25

The rain had certainly done its job. The awful fire was out, the Woodlands seemed greener than ever, and Babs's poor bottom had well and truly cooled off.

The animals gathered in front of Hedgequarters, the WI6 mission control. H and her twin sister Henrietta, the infamous Highway Hedgehog, stood on a large tree stump.

'Ahem!' H began, getting the crowd's attention. 'I would like to start by welcoming our friends from New Pineland ... AS NEW CITIZENS OF THE UNITED WOODLANDS.'

'HURRAH!' A big cheer erupted from the excited animals.

'And also, a heartfelt thank you to the brave WI6 team who solved this great pickle.'

'YAAAARRR!' The crowd cheered enthusiastically as Mole, Nutter and Doorkins, with Muriel perched on his shoulder, shuffled awkwardly on to the tree stump platform.

'Go Doorkins!' yelled Pippin, hanging from a tree with her bat family. Doorkins gave a little embarrassed wave back.

Henrietta solemnly hung a silver acorn award around each of their necks, with a special diddy one for the little moth. H then waved her paws for quiet.

'And for outstanding bravery in the line of duty and, er, a rather unusual weasel rain dance that saved us all, the golden acorn goes to ...' H sighed deeply and shook her head. 'AGENT WEASEL!'

WHACK
HOORAY

The crowd went wild. There was cheering and yelping, loud enough it felt like the earth beneath them shook. But Weasel did not appear.

'Where is he?' mumbled H impatiently. 'First he refuses to untie me and now he stands us up at his own award ceremony, it's just too much!'

Mole just shrugged. She had no idea where Weasel had got to.

'YOOO-HOO!' came a loud cry from the landing pad on top of HQ. There stood Agent Weasel, and attached to his back were the most magnificent pair of wings – WI6 wings!

'TALLY-HO!' he cried, launching himself from the platform in a death-defying leap.

'Uh-oh!' said Doorkins and the animals covered their eyes in fear for their friend. But after a second or two, there was no SPLAT! sound, and they dared to take a peek.

Weasel swooped down to the ground in a graceful glide. He landed right on top of the tree stump, next to his friends.

Everybody cheered.

'You'll be giving me flying lessons next, don't you know?' chuckled Captain Barney-Barnster from the front of the crowd. Weasel gave his friend a cheeky wink.

'Well, what a marvellous entrance,' said Henrietta, admiring the pair of wings jealously.

'Yes, those clever Boffin Bunnies made 'em up from spare pigeon feathers. Brilliant, aren't they?' replied Weasel. He beamed with pride.

'I could rule the Woodlands with those wings!' she murmured under her breath.

'What was that?' asked Weasel.

'Oh, nothing. Here's your golden acorn. Well done!'

The proud WI6 spy stepped forward to receive his sparkly trinket and the crowd went wild.

'YAY for whatshisname!' cried Granny Weasel, clapping along. Weasel raised his eyebrows and shook his head.

'Now all the formalities are over,' announced H, 'Chef Flourplop has a fine celebration spread in the HQ canteen. Including tea, cake and biscuits – all are welcome.'

Everyone cheered even louder, if that's possible!

'Well, another adventure comes to an end, old chum,' said Weasel to his best buddy, Doorkins, as the pair strolled towards the HQ.

'Yes, those wings would have been handy, though, don't you think?' replied the little dormouse.

'THE WINGS!' cried Weasel. 'I was only borrowing them! I'd better get them back to those Boffin Bunnies, or I'll be for it!'

'I'll come with you!' Doorkins said.

After a quick scurry, the friends arrived back at the tree stump, but the wings had gone!

'Where on earth—?'

Weasel's ponderings were cut off by a loud holler.

'YEEEEEHAA!'

The pair looked up. There, against the bright blue sky, was the Highway Hedgehog wearing Weasel's wings.

'I'M THE KING OF THE WORLD!' she cried

gleefully. She flew up and down and did a loop-de-loop and, with a loud CRUNCH!, flew straight into the trunk of a very wide oak tree.

There was a loud groan and she slid slowly to the ground.

'S-stand and d-d-deliver,' croaked the dazed hedgehog to no one in particular.

'Ouch.' Weasel cringed with a shudder, before turning to his friend. 'Er … tea, cake and biscuits, my friend?'

'Y-yes, tea, cake and biscuits,' agreed Doorkins.

And the two friends sloped off, arm in arm.

LOOK OUT FOR

-NICK EAST-
I ♥ WI6
AGENT WEASEL
AND THE ABOMINABLE DR SNOW

-NICK EAST-
I ♥ W.I.6
AGENT WEASEL
AND THE ROBBER KING

NICK EAST is the illustrator of the bestselling *Toto the Ninja Cat* as well as the *Goodnight Digger* and *Knock Knock* series. He worked for many years as a museum designer but has always been a storyteller, whether as a child, filling sketchbooks with quirky characters, or as a designer displaying a collection of ancient artefacts. He lives near York with his wife and two children and, when not writing or drawing, he is out roaming the countryside with a rucksack on his back.